The Two Doctors Górski

D0068340

THE TWO
DOCTORS GÓRSKI

ISAAC FELLMAN

A TOM DOHERTY ASSOCIATES BOOK

NEW YORK

This is a work of fiction. All of the characters, organizations, and events portrayed in this novella are either products of the author's imagination or are used fictitiously.

THE TWO DOCTORS GÓRSKI

Cover design by FORT

A Tordotcom Book
Published by Tom Doherty Associates
120 Broadway
New York, NY 10271

www.tor.com

ISBN 978-1-250-84012-7 (ebook)
ISBN 978-1-250-84093-6 (trade paperback)

First Edition: 2022

For Waverly

The Two Doctors Górski

Chapter 1

They all warned her about Marec Górski. The bursar's assistant and the registrar's assistant and the dean's assistant converged around her like the three witches that they were, and they told her the same thing:

"Dr. Górski is one of our best." ("One of our best.") "But he is from an older generation. He's a traditionalist in how he does things." ("He's older, and he can be conservative.") "So you'll need to be a little careful in how you present yourself." ("How you present your work to him.") "You wouldn't have got in here if you weren't very good, and he'll see that for himself if you just *be* yourself." ("And don't try to impress him.")

To be careful! These people didn't know Annae Hofstader, didn't know how *careful* she was, at every moment except for the moments when she snapped and let loose all care, flung herself half-crooked into disaster's wet mouth, simply because caring never made enough of a difference. They didn't know how she researched each thing she did, how well she had already been warned about Marec. He had been too great in his time not to be awful today, and then, of course, there was the matter of Ariel. First-year graduate students in dark bars still debated the ethics of Ariel; second-years knew better than to admit they were still obsessed.

And yet they insisted on warning her. Oh, she was used to being handed pills like this, compounded of patronization and preemptive blame, with a coating of good advice, just to make you doubt yourself if you hesitated for a moment to take them. If she was in Britain now instead of California, the only difference was the design. But the truth was that they didn't poison her anymore. She had built up too high a tolerance.

Still, she couldn't resist the thrill of being warned. It made her feel like an astronaut strapping in, or a soldier loading out. The adrenaline of the drop, floating high above some heady city, your parachute packed by unknown hands, the safety off on your gun, your hands and lips tingling with panic. She was prepared to be afraid of Marec, because she was already afraid of everyone; she'd had practice. What more did he have to offer her in the night market of fear, when she was the richest woman in the world and already owned it all?

But, well. Despite all of it, there was magic attached to his name. Not real magic, but ordinary magic, a medieval touch that illuminated the initial *M* and *G* with red and gold. He had been great and he had been finished at thirty, like all the great ones, and there was a magic in that too. The lure of him was the lure of any finished thing: you could look at him and see his full story, with ending.

~

For the first session of the graduate seminar, she wore a brownish lipstick, and her classiest skirt with the big plaid and no elastic, and a shawl she'd knitted from yarn with a dull sugary sparkle, in a pattern designed to look like human DNA. Then she'd taken the shawl off. It was an affectation for the old Annae, the one who had always tried to please—others, and herself. The skirt was dangerously close to being affected too, with its velvet ribbon trim, but it was also uncomfortable, which showed that she was a serious person.

Here, she told herself, she would please no one. She would aim herself at Brandford University, finish her thesis, and then escape with her PhD like a rocket fired out of orbit, evading every empty thing until it came to the greatest emptiness of all. Then she would finally be done.

~

The seminar was in one of those fairy-tale rooms you found at Brandford, walls and ceiling shaped by Victorian trowels that might as well have been Tudor, and a small window of uneven latticework. It smelled like the underfunded library of Annae's youth, something that made it somehow even more English, damply redolent of Pullman and Pratchett. The table was too large for the claustrophobic space, and the graduate students around it were all young men in Oxfam suits. She sat down, safe but too visible in her heavy bangs and all her woolen clothes. And then Marec Górski came in, and the air in the room sucked into him and vanished.

He went into his lecture before his jacket was unbuttoned, before his bag was down. He was seventy, looked eighty, and wore a loose academic gown as if his body had lain desiccating in it by a remote roadside since the summer term. His lightly fuzzed head was held a bit askew, which completed the picture of a fallen cyclist, neck broken.

"Magic has remained etymologically the same for millennia," he said — voice rough but surprisingly high, a sandpapered choirboy. "Old French *magique,* Latin *magice,* Greek *magike,* Old Persian *magush.* What does this suggest about human beings?"

He edged himself around the table, put down his briefcase at its head, looked around the room as if balancing all of them on his tongue. Slowly, almost pityingly, he went on. "That we've always known what magic is, whether or not it was understood at the time, whether or not it was considered a superstition or a lie. Those two syllables endure. They're as hardwired as those almost onomatopoeic Anglo-Saxon words, 'dog' or 'food.' Magic is more intuitive to human thought than literature. It's more intuitive than mathematics. Magic is not a hard science. It is a soft field that takes the impressions of everything that encounters it, and uses them to get stronger. Magic is also the only conscious field of study. The only one that talks back."

He stopped talking as abruptly as he had started and snapped open his briefcase. From it he withdrew a sharp stack of papers and a china coffee mug filled to a quarter inch below the brim. The thick, bodily smell of coffee filled the room and steamed the windows.

"You know me. I was once near great," he said. "*Near* great, I say, because fine though my career was, I never found *my theme*. Melville said that a great book requires a mighty theme. I had the brains and the drive, but not the inspiration. The best thing I ever made was a person, but most of us make people, in the end. I could have done better. I won't settle for anything less in my graduate students than inspiration, yet so far, I have never encountered it once. None of you seems likely to change that record. Remind me which ones you are? And you"—indicating Annae—"you'll be last."

The men in Oxfam suits gave him their names and then, with more prodding, their interests. She tried to make note of the names—Peter, Joshua, Thomas, Gordon, Torquil—but couldn't connect them to their faces; it was like one of those quizzes you take in primary school, where you have a list of men and a list of achievements and you have to connect them up. Thomas Edison and the light bulb, Benjamin Franklin and electricity. Perhaps there was something contagious in Górski's indifference, or perhaps they had done their best to become interchangeable.

Górski said, "Now, Annie."

She straightened up and said, "Annae, An*nay*."

"Nay, Annae," he said. "The plural of Anna? How did you come by that?"

"My parents wanted something unique."

"Ah, yes. The American mania for customization."

"Maybe," she said, and drew back the corner of her mouth until a dimple appeared. "I'm sure English parents make up names too."

"And what is your field of study, Annas?"

"Mental illness and trauma."

"Interesting. Are you pro or con?"

"Well," said Annae, "without wanting to put an ethical burden on the idea of being sick or traumatized—"

"Not at all. I am the last man to put an ethical burden

on anyone. But, Annae, I was making a joke." A gentle lift to the eyebrows, an assurance that nothing could be kinder. "The trouble with curing mental illness is that there are so many more of them now. It's a moving target. When I was a young man, people did not become manic; they *burnt hot.*"

"I've met some people who were manic," said Annae, hearing her voice slide higher, "and it's not heat, exactly—"

"I knew a boy who was taken away for it," said Marec, "when I was your age. How old are you? You look fourteen."

"I'm twenty-seven."

"Ah," he said. "The age when all the musicians die. You are not a musician?"

"No."

"Then that's all right." Marec cleared his throat. "Do you really suppose that you can do it?"

"I don't know," she said. "I want to spend my whole career trying."

"A sound bite," said Marec, "verily, a sound bite. You *are* an American. In a few months you'll be emailing me to talk about 'wrapping up the term.'"

"Has that happened before?"

"Twice," he said, and there was a knowing, stifled laugh from Gordon or Torquil, one of the Scots.

"Well, I'm sure they had their reasons."

"It's funny," he said. "You look like such an English rose, but then you open your mouth."

"American Beauty rose," chimed in Gordon-or-Torquil. Annae blushed, not from flattery, but from confusion, and the room laughed. If she had ever thought of herself as a rose, it would be a withered one—crisp, dry, delicate. But it was impossible to articulate the thought beyond that image, especially with the laughter gasping at her from everywhere.

"Which is French," said Górski. "A French cultivar. You should know that, Torquil; you're a botanist."

"I don't know my individual roses," said Torquil.

"Maybe that's your problem," said Górski. "*Anno, annas, annat.*"

~

Torquil followed her out of the room after the lecture and stood contritely in the damp sunlight outside, after she'd refolded her wet umbrella. He said, "That was rude, I'm sorry."

"You don't need to apologize," she said, and thought: *That only calls attention to it.* Her fingers folded up in their thin leather gloves.

"But I would like to. Sometimes I just free-associate.

It's a thing for which I am known."

"Then apology accepted," she said, and turned to walk away.

"Wait," he said, and kept pace with her, his stride lengthening. "You need to get out while you can. I mean it. Whatever your reasons for coming here, I guarantee they're not as good as the reasons to leave. Do you realize he makes a show of having us introduce ourselves every year? There's always the five of us and one American girl that he expects to be grateful."

"Perhaps I am grateful," she said.

"Are you quite sure you're American? I never heard an American say 'perhaps.'"

"Of course I am."

"Why are you grateful?"

To her it had the feeling of a Zen koan: some crucial word missing. Does a dog have Buddha nature? Or the Marx brothers: What's the difference between a duck? "I had a bad time in my previous program," she told him, her head and mouth full of air. "It wasn't the best fit for me."

"Oh," he said, a little too wisely.

"You *know* my reasons for being here, don't you? You've Googled."

"No," he said, although there was a narrowing about his eyes. The rain started again, a slow rain that hissed through the trees and didn't drown out the cars. She could hear their motors just over the high, well-shaped berm, like the bone of a hill, that was supposed to block the road. The narrowing in his eyes really was quite pronounced, a soft tension that showed you what he'd look like in twenty years. Despite herself, she liked his taut young face, which had the capability for disguise but not for affectation. His Oxfam suit was brown, but not brown tweed.

"The job didn't end well," said Annae. "As a result of which I'm in no position to negotiate. I'm well aware Dr. Górski is a hard bargain—"

"You can call him Marec. He prefers it anyway, and it's half as many syllables wasted."

She put her umbrella back up. Torquil didn't have one; he put up the collar of his jacket and made a grimace, and she raised the umbrella up to cover him too. The hard dirt of the path around them barely seemed penetrated by the rain. The shadows of his face were softened by the umbrella, his body close—then the smell of him, exhaled from the drooping collar of his shirt, that familiar deodorant, the black-and-white bottle and the name vaguely reminiscent of Vichy France, the smell of Jonathon's house. The perverse nostalgia of it. Under the layers of insults, under the cruel emails, under the private harshness of Jonathon's manner, there lay the earliest tight-furled memories of his house, before everything had gone wrong, when his house had felt like a refuge from everything. A humming fridge full of expensive treats, wine in pink cans, rosemary and cheese; the quiet lights caught in the gray carpets; the smell of the right products for his skin and hair.

A tiny voice somewhere near the top of her skull asked: *Why this? Why now? How is it so easy to bring you so low? Surely it isn't this obvious—a smell and then a feeling; a feeling and then the pop of a flashbulb or a bullet, and the smell of something burning out? Surely you are not so simple a creature as this?* Then she closed her eyes, feeling once again the mortification of that final onslaught, of standing at the sink washing perfectly good oil and pepper out of a salad bowl, the sleeves of her vintage angora sweater getting sopping wet, as Jonathon told her in the kindest possible terms that he was done with her childishness and desperation to be loved, tired of humoring her intellectual pretensions, tired of pretending her work was serious—

How she had let the bowl fill up with warm water, then seized magic and heated it to boiling around her fingers—

Mortification, Latin, *to make dead*—

Torquil was still there, somehow. He must have said something. He was looking at her, pinched and expectant. And all of a sudden there was nothing to do but to rip open a little corner of his mind and slip inside, to look at herself through his eyes, because she could not bear to be Annae anymore, and because he probably deserved it.

~

Torquil shuddered in his skin. Her look in that moment sank too deep into him. He looked down at her too, the skin stretched taut but matte over her cheekbones, the bend of her elbow in its pressed blouse, the hair a shining solid mass, like hair in a movie. A too-perfect woman, with nothing the eye could catch on, as if all the obvious work of perfecting her appearance were not toward the purpose of beauty, but of invisibility. She was a feast for Marec, someone so well put together that she had surely learned it from being taken apart.

~

"Are you all right?" she asked him. She had jerked out of his mind suddenly, because it had been so unsoothing—it had been sharp in her mouth, it had tasted bad. A bath of anxiety, with stagnant water and green flotsam beneath its surfaces.

"I'm fine," he said, and attempted a quirk of a smile, the corner of his mouth twitching like a live wire. "It's been a long day. A day with Marec is a day without sunshine."

"How did you start working with him?"

"He charmed me," Torquil said quietly, the wind playing with his thin hair. "*He* wanted to work with *me*. God knows why. Look, Annae, I have looked you up, all right? I wanted to know who would be joining us."

"So you've seen the article."

"Yes," he said.

"And what did you think?"

He blew air out of his mouth and she plunged into his mind again, this time feeling as if she were yanking handfuls of it away. The sheer frustration, the weariness of this moment.

~

Think? Think? He'd Googled her late the previous night, the unusual name having been familiar. Then he'd dug deeper and deeper, fascinated and depressed. All that seemed to have nothing to do with the woman in front of him now, who was once again giving him that look, that brass thumbtack of a look that pinned him crisply up. A cautionary tale, the article. About the dangers of elevating people too soon in their careers, lest they prove flashes or frauds.

In a video from a morning news show, a much younger Annae—bangs longer, makeup darker, the red of her sweater bleeding through her thin white lab coat—had demonstrated something shocking: removal of fear in the rat. She showed how she'd trained them to be frightened of a red laser-pointer dot, then explained the little tweak—just a small nudge to the electrical pattern of the brain, based on Taylor's work with spine and nerve pain—that made it go away. Torquil was a plant specialist and did no work with animal physiology; all he could tell was that the work was either a massive step forward from Taylor's fairly basic 1980s experiments, or a step that had nothing to do with them at all, done by a thinker so original that any attempt at citation was basically a falsehood. Annae stroked the rats' little heads, and then—presto—no fear! They had chased the dot like kittens.

"They don't live long afterward," Annae had explained apologetically to the audience. "Work like this always has consequences for the body; the change in the charge poisons the system, and it breeds cancer or anemia. The real brass ring for a scientist like me is to turn it into something else—some harmless chemical that I can drain off. But with magic like this, it would theoretically be possible to edit our response to trauma, to cure mental illness of all kinds—just a little change in the way we feel, and that makes all the difference."

The country had been briefly fascinated by Annae, who was an undergraduate at the time and had a shy grin of which there was no evidence now. A certain kind of science writing had clustered around her, the kind that takes the scientist's simplification and simplifies it further—a little change in the way we feel! How simple, how graspable, how elegant. Perhaps it really could be done. Torquil had felt the pull of the demonstration too, imagining his life without antidepressants, without anti-anxiety drugs, without their side effects and long trial periods, imagining himself changed with one clean stroke. The thought was dystopian—but how appealing it was, as dystopias are.

But then Annae had fallen silent. It seemed that things weren't that simple after all. And then this article had surfaced, heavily quoting her former supervisor, Jonathon Bayer. Annae had been raised too high and too quickly. She had only had one idea, and that an incomplete one. "To be honest," Bayer had said, "I think that it was partly because she was a woman, and everyone wanted a woman to come along to save advanced magic from being such a boys' club. That doesn't mean that the right woman couldn't excel in this field, or rather that many women could not. But everyone wanted Annae to be another Meril Meyerfeld—they wanted to see gravity reversed—and that's not her. The only reason I don't call her a fraud is that I sincerely think she believes that she's a genius."

Torquil had looked at her Facebook, to see if it seemed like a fraud's Facebook. Bayer was all over it. He was youngish, good-looking, with a square face and an expansive look. In one photo he had his arm slung around her shoulders. She was wearing a white shirtdress, very crisp, and dragged to greater crispness by the tightness of his grip on her shoulder. When you scrolled past him, all that was left was the kind of Facebook page that's staccato and mostly full of other people's happy-birthdays, photos of Annae at parties with women she didn't appear to know well. He'd scrolled to the very bottom, to the formation of Annae's account. But there was nothing there except a note that she had been born.

"What do you think?"

All of this had gone by in a moment, a microdot of thought. He felt his face convulse, compress. She looked mildly horrified, as if she had seen everything he'd thought, everything he was thinking now, every nasty misogynistic intrusive thought about the way the girls in the photos had looked like dead sunflowers, the way they would gangle and stretch. Their raw skin under the flash. All the ways he'd believed Bayer's words, because Torquil, a known fraud, believed in frauds.

"I think you're hard done by," he said to her quietly. "And I think you should watch out for Marec, anyway. No doubt you've been warned that he's unkind, and obviously he is that, but it's worse. He will either try to stop you from ever leaving this place, or destroy your career entirely."

"I don't have a choice," she told him, flinging the words suddenly into his face. "Don't you know? Marec is the only

one who'd take me. Leave me alone. Don't pretend you don't
know everything."

"Know everything? I don't know anything. I'm—I'm
sorry. I'll go."

~

Annae sat on the bus, her face in her hands, locked in
dread and humiliation, wondering what she was doing
here. It would have been so easy to leave academia, to
leave magic. She had thought that she could bear anything, after leaving Jonathon and losing her position; she
had thought herself numb, finished, after the tenth or
twentieth long email, *I see now that I was wrong to think
you were anything more than a spoiled child,* after he had
complained of her personality and her appearance until
she felt like a muddy blur, something pummeled and un-
recognizable; after she had finally tried to ask the department to keep him away from her, only to find herself
asked to leave campus herself. But she had found that she
could not bear losing her life's work.

She tried to feel the bus seat beneath her, the ridged
floor under her feet. She took a deep breath, trying to
steady herself, to establish herself. But it was like trying
to stay awake when the alarm rang but the sleeping pill
hadn't worn off. You were always pulled back under, back

in, to the black heat just outside of your consciousness, to the place where Jonathon waited to lash another strip of her away.

~

At home, she should have cooked dinner, but she couldn't face the gas stove. She lay on the couch instead and gathered a shaggy cushion to her chest, reaching behind her to unzip the top inch of her skirt. She longed for the wafting escape from herself, which ever since Jonathon she had wanted more than scholarship or food. Her old mainstays, the favorite minds she'd read just to get away, were back in America and hopelessly out of her range: the man who worked at the bakery, the vet she'd watched with her cats. Minds like soothing YouTube videos, ASMR.

She liked reading because it made the world feel like a book written in unlimited third-person perspective, her favorite since the fantasy novels of her childhood, whose chapters traded names and narrators with the avidity of little girls swapping dolls or Pokémon. To the skilled reader, the world was just one narrator after another. Sometimes she wondered if anyone was reading *her*, and imagined herself saying, in some way, take it, you're welcome to it, it's little enough use to me.

She let herself drift back to Torquil. He was stressful to be with, but he was the only person here whose mind she knew.

~

Torquil went home, made himself a cup of coffee, and sat down at the long lab bench he used as a desk. It was of sweet reclaimed wood, covered in a long row of plants turned toward the window or toward the door or toward different parts of him. The plants soothed him, and he felt the relaxation in his heart and muscles and lungs, as if each trumpeting flower and unfurling leaf was sending out a ray of heat. People terrified Torquil; plants gave him rest.

He was watching the video of Annae again. She seemed so bright and shivering, thrilled to be here, to be sharing what she'd made. He struggled to reconcile her with the woman he'd met today, who had seemed, in important ways, dead— dried and still, all the water pressed out of her. She was talking about bringing more girls into magic. Then there was a mention of Jonathon Bayer, with a ping of excitement in her voice like a text coming in. This woman was in love with this man, and in love with her work; she wanted to be a mentor the way some happily partnered people want to have children, because they hope it will make their happy thoughts concrete.

It seemed to him that American magicians had to be very driven. They only taught simple magic in school over there, not much beyond transmogrification of plants. He had seen videos of giggling twelfth graders turning a palm leaf into an air plant, but it was the kind of air plant that looks a lot like a palm leaf. Torquil had had an English education, and so he knew magic, knew it like he knew the bones running up his trouser legs. He knew it with a quiet tranquility that half rhymed with his name, troubled though he felt about everything else in life. Leaping the gulf between that American school-magic and the real stuff was like leaping the gulf between calculus and the kind of swooning math that they made Oscar-bait movies about.

Christ Jesus—he needed to eat. Cooking was hard for Torquil, because he had some very strong feelings about plants. He spent hours with them every day, teasing them at a cellular level, flicking at their DNA. When it came time to chop them with a crude, granular knife (for like all magicians, Torquil looked at the world in extreme close-up)— when it came time to sizzle and sear them in a pan, and watch them curl away, he got depressed and had to go to bed after dinner. Meat was even worse.

Someone had once asked him why he cooked his veg, why he didn't just eat salad. Torquil had had to think about that a little, and then had said, "It's because it's a painless kill. A kind of euthanasia for them. The knife and the heat. At least

I don't have to bite *them to death."*
  "But they're already dead, Torquil."
  "I know that."

~

Annae found herself still on the couch, staring groggily at the dark. She sat up with a groan of pain, a muscle in her neck spasming, and then went to the kitchen to shovel something into her numb mouth, crackers and cheese and some grapes, all of it good. They said British food was bad, but to her it tasted like Tolkien food, the laws that protected its quality stiffer and higher than American laws, so that everything was salty and sweet and rich, a still life in a bite. *Vanitas.* When she was done, she went straight to the bedroom, released herself from the crumpled heat of her sweater and skirt and from the scratchy tension of her bra, and paused, sitting down on the edge of the bed.

Her apartment was in a new building, and it could have been anywhere: America, even, with its glassy coolness, its cheap wall-to-wall. The window was covered with a sheet of cardboard, for although she had bought a dry chenille bedspread and a white bed of a Styrofoam stiffness, and a set of plastic drawers for her things, she had forgotten curtains. She liked the anonymity—it was as if nobody lived here—

but wished it could have been pushed further, that she had been a person who needed no sofa, no bed, no body. The person who had plunged into the delicately scented bloom of Jonathon's sheets, who had loved the feeling of his hundred-dollar pillow across the back of her skull, had gone away, and she didn't know where.

She looked down at her thigh and, with a slight twitch of her fingers across the dry skin, she made one of her blotches. Tiny bumps like eczema, and then a larger papule that grew under the pad of her thumb. When she did this, she felt the nodes of her brain, clear and flowing. Annae had cut herself as a teenager, in just this part of the thigh. She still had the scars, as long and thin and untidy as uncombed hairs. Halfway through her relationship with Jonathon, she had found the irresistible urge coming up again, for by then he had begun to critique all that she did, crossing her out with a firm hand as if she were an undergraduate making the same grammar mistakes again and again on a paper. This time, she had discovered the blotches, the blemishes, which she thought were better, for no one could see them; she lacked the skill to make them permanent, being a specialist after all in the brain. It was harm reduction, really. They faded when she stopped paying attention to them, and by morning they were gone. In the meantime, they soothed her. The irritation under the surface never quite broke through and bled, but that was all right. It was worth it for the absolute privacy.

She could make a light patch on the corner of her mouth, just above the chin. A pink hot patch on her cheek. Eczema on her elbows; a big dark rash on her stomach. When she was too tired to go on, she went to bed under the chenille and watched squares of light sail past in the dark, the lights of cars or hallucinations. Annae always hallucinated after doing magic, even if only a little; it was what happened when you pulled the brain out of alignment.

She had told herself for some time that her mind-reading was a matter of self-protection, and then that it was for science. Lately, she had been working on telling herself that it was for revenge, although on whom she could not say, for it harmed no one who had harmed her. But really, she knew she did it because it offered a comfort that nothing else could provide, not alcohol and not shopping— which in any case were instruments for fitting in with other people, and not the sources of any private pleasure.

The comfort of mind-reading was not the comfort of Jonathon's sheets, the comfort of money and stability. Other people's minds were grimy, worn out, clogged with decay. But when she was inside someone else's mind, she didn't feel the world biting into her. She didn't feel like a fraud. She felt nothing at all, except what they were feeling; she could see her face reacting to them sometimes, but the emotions behind it were as inscrutable as those of a stranger. And she loved knowing she was illegible to people, loved the safety it offered. She saw herself clean and tidy, well dressed, her hair straightened, nothing torn or shrunken or translucent that ought not to be, an attentive listener with perfectly opaque eyes.

She had told a soon-to-be-ex-therapist about this once, back in San Cipriano, pretending the actual mind-reading was only skilled empathy and attention, because actual mind-reading was wildly unethical. The therapist had said gently, "It sounds as if you can't get into your *own* head, Annae, and that's what should concern us." Annae had said, "Don't *tell* me what should concern me. Don't *tell* me how to think."

She lay awake for hours before she could sleep. Well, it had been barely after dinnertime when she lay down; that was to be expected. She tried to read some research on her phone, Otono's new work on adjusting the perception of risk and reward in the rhesus macaque. It was an incredibly exciting paper that only made her feel anxious, because it was the sort of thing she should be doing, but Otono had rejected her along with everyone else except Marec.

Finally she closed her eyes and decided to look into Marec himself. Surely he would be such a challenge to read that he would exhaust her into insensibility. She couldn't take Torquil's clench of anxiety anymore, and somehow she suspected that Marec was never anxious.

She was afraid of what he might have thought of her, but Annae loved ripping off Band-Aids, popping pimples, breaking scabs. It was impossible to resist the urge to know someone who might think ill of her. She closed her eyes, looked for the pattern of his mind, found it.

∼

Marec loved to come home late. The silence of the lanes through which he pedaled, the faint hint of wildlife in the grass, the scatter of light on dense English lawns, made the world seem a more focused creation than it was. He braked his bicycle as he pulled up to the cottage, pausing for a moment to admire it: the quiet hulk of the building, the thatch fitting like a close warm hood. He had built the place himself decades ago. It was a relief to return home to something he had made, something that was entirely his, whose very plaster bore the imprint and showed the span of his hands. From here you could not see the town at all, only the tower of the cathedral, and that had been dug out of the wet earth of the hills nine hundred years ago; the color of it fit the land. He let go of his spattered bicycle and went inside, glancing at the fireplace to light a fire.

He cracked his long back. The fireplace warmed the whole room: close walls in marshmallow white, the trestle table that had so awed and horrified Torquil Gibson, who had said it was like looking at slabs of meat fitted together. Why had he ever invited Gibson here? High-strung, silly, a keen nibbler at ideas. And he smoked, although he said he did not. Not so sympathetic to plants then, was he?

His fingers traced the raised veins of the wood, varnished raw from the tree. He felt the dead life in them, under the dirt, under the gloss. Even now there was something, cells and pulp. No, he was not to think about Gibson now. And Annae Hofstader tired him out too. Had they been unable to commit to "Anne" or "Anna"? Just like Jennifer, exactly like. Tiny girls, too soft to break.

He should have kept the students from the house from the start, not just Gibson. He needed one place where he was entirely private, where he was entirely himself, free of others' voices. The flesh of this place was his flesh. The students didn't see it, always commented in polite surprise on the clash of his home and his name—as if a man with a Polish father must be genetically immune to the charms of English vernacular architecture. Well, his mother was English as dirt, and he claimed as much of a right to that dirt and its products as anyone.

Yes, Marec thought. Live among your ideas; live among your memories. Live in a house that's the product of your body, and don't let anyone into it. If he'd known that before Ariel happened, Marec would never have lost him. Never let *any precious thing go.*

He took his cell phone from his jacket pocket and tossed it on the table as if he were tossing it at Gibson, hoping to see him fumble it in his long hands, drop it to the ground. It lit up with messages and emails, and he opened a bag of bread, scowling down at the red numbers. How did he have five new emails since leaving the office? Would these people never stop digging at him, as if mining his skin and muscles for bits of precious material? With toast on the fork over the fire, he thumbed the button that would let him read them.

From: Jonathon Bayer <jonathon.bayer@sancipriano.edu>
To: Marec Górski <mgorsk@brandford.ac.uk>

Dear Dr. Gorski,

Jonathon Bayer here, of the University of California, San Cipri-ano. I'm writing to you on a matter of some urgency, and I hope you'll forgive me for taking so long to do so. I did not know that the student in question was working with you until today.

First of all, please let me say that I am a great admirer of your work. Although I am anything but an elementalist myself—I am in medical magic, a nerve specialist—I have followed all that you do for many years, from The Eternal Flame *on through your more recent, and spectacular, work on realigning jet streams. I hope you don't think me a flat-*

terer when I say it's possibly the most significant body of work to come from a living magician.

The reason I write is because, as I said, I've become aware that Annae Hofstader has come to your department to complete her PhD. As you probably know, Annae began her work here at San Cipriano, where I was her PhD supervisor. I was surprised to learn that Annae will be completing her degree. I found her to be a consistently unreliable student, emotionally unstable, manipulative, and unable to take criticism. There is a more sensitive matter, as well: Annae and I were in a romantic relationship for the several years that she was in the program. I trust that you will be discreet about this knowledge, especially to Annae herself, and I realize that in many ways it reflects very poorly on me. I should have had the judgment not to succumb to a student's romantic attentions. You know how they become obsessed with us—well, we preside over their whole world; how could they not? But ethically, I know I should never have said yes. The truth is that Annae can be very charming when it suits her, and of course she is a beautiful woman as well. When it comes to such charms—poured liberally over one's head by someone who presents herself as a kind of anointing shrine maiden of science—I am as weak as any other man who has spent his life in the laboratory and the library.

Our relationship ended badly. Annae left me abruptly, without explaining why. She then tried to slander my name to others in the department, accusing me of being the one who had seduced her. The overwhelming impression was of someone who demands to speak to life's manager after not being given the bargain she knows she deserves. I now suspect that the relationship began as a way of getting Annae through her degree despite her significant deficits as a scientist and as a human being. If that's so, she did not succeed, and it has left her with a poor professional reputation that apparently has not followed her overseas.

I take no pleasure in writing all of this, and hope I haven't gone on too long or given the impression of simply airing a grievance. I wanted to warn you to be on your guard around this woman, not to give in to her blandishments, and not to believe her flattery. With a good deal of time and very hard work on both of your parts, she may yet prove a good magician with a good career ahead of her. She is, however, not a person I wish to know, and I take comfort in the fact that I no longer do. For the sake of your ability to focus on your work, which I know is something you (rightly) value over all else, I would advise you to limit your contact.

Cheers,

Jonathon Bayer
Jules F. Muir Chair in Neuromancy
University of California, San Cipriano

In a fury Marec flipped open his laptop, planted his hands on the home row, and rapidly typed:

Sir,

Like all Americans, you have an affinity for large words cruelly misused; "blandishments" and "flattery" are redundant. I would expect you to know that difference of all differences, as you flatter me shamelessly in your second paragraph. You understand my work not at all. I don't know why magicians so often labour under the delusion that, because we are all magicians, we can be conversant with one another's research. In the other sciences, people have the sense to stay apart. No physician ever assumed that he could understand the research of a physicist, unless of course he was a very great fool. If you did understand my work, you would understand its poverty both of purpose and of execution. The greatest "tell" is, of course, that you don't mention Ariel. All of my admirers admire me for but one reason—my work with Ariel—and none of you have the simple courage to mention him. What does it say about someone when he is only admired by cowards?

As for the matter of Annae Hofstader, you'll not tell me how to manage my own graduate students. They are a sickly enough group of people without my giving them that much attention. I don't care what you may have done with Miss

Hofstader or how it made you feel. You obviously belong together in the sense that her name sounds like a set of specialized organs, and yours sounds like a charity telethon to raise money for distressed Jons. Do not contact me again.

Marec Górski
P.S. "CHEERS"?

He slammed the laptop shut, smelling burnt toast; his first thought was that he was having a stroke, so furious was the bubble of rage within him, but then he remembered and pulled the fork out of the fire, too angry to eat now anyway. He yanked the bread from its sharp tip, but that wasn't enough; he threw the bread in the general direction of the kitchen, but that wasn't enough; he finally threw the fork to the floor, and that wasn't enough, but he was sweating, exhausted, the color burning out his cheeks.

Why was he like this? He felt Ariel's absence like something cauterized. Ariel could have explained it all to him— he would have taken Marec in his grip and told him the truth, for he always did. And before they had separated, Ariel would have done even better; he would have prevented Marec from growing so angry at all. God, he was shedding tears. He dragged his sleeve over his eyes, baffled at their fall.

All Marec wanted was to be left alone. Why was that so difficult? Why could one person with very simple needs not be *left alone to do his work? He knew he could still do it—had sacrificed Ariel to give himself the space to do it—had given everything up, just for the work, and yet it seemed that he would die without realizing it, that molten potential he had shown at twenty-five and thirty. Of all the things one could want, why could he not even have himself?*

One thing was quite certain though: he had a problem. If Bayer was lying about Annae, then he would have to help her, have to defend her, when he didn't even know the fucking woman. If Bayer was telling the truth, well, then! He had known from the first faux smile, the first dimple she'd allowed, that she was a simpering little shapeshifter. No, one way or the other, he would need to press those smiles out of her.

~

Annae gave a pained cry and buried her face in the pillow.

Marec Górski had been her hero when she was ten. He remained Jonathon's hero to this day. Jonathon had admired him because he thought he was an Übermensch, and she had admired him because he had written a wonderful book about magic for children called *Twelve Theorems*. She could still remember the bliss of reading it, like the bliss of licking the crystallized salt from the inside of the microwave popcorn bag: finally, here was a pleasure for her alone. She had read it again and again, into middle school, through high school, and more surreptitiously in college. Twelve short animal fables, each of which posed a problem in magic. They called on her to be subtle and quick, but above all empathetic. The pain of others was presented as a problem that could be managed, if you cared enough. She didn't think until later about what kind of person might want to tell another, "If you could care, you could manage me."

She knew of Marec's reputation, and knew that, however bad it was, he was still out of her league. But there she was, applying to work under him, *because fuck Jonathon*, because she would prove to him that his idol thought her worthy, that she did not have a child's understanding of magic after all. And then there she'd been, rejected by everyone else, for she had no letter of recommendation, no findings, no future. And then, finally, there she'd been: in a McDonald's in San Cipriano, composing the acceptance letter with her eyes blurred by grease and tears, telling herself, *I choose him, he doesn't choose me.*

Chapter 2

She woke in the night, sweat breaking through her skin. Deep in the town, she could sense something unnatural, something magically caused—a fire. She knew it the way you know the location of your own hand, your own knees; the way you know where gunfire was coming from. Now the smell was reaching her, creeping through the insulation of the window. She threw off the bedclothes and went to look out.

No ambiguity there: it was the tower of Brandford Cathedral, flipped open to reveal fire like the stitching of muscle under skin. With her eyes on it, she could feel the explosion of magic all the more forcefully, something hungry, ugly, very wrong. This wasn't the report of a gun. It was more like a nuclear bomb, and like a physicist, Annae knew the exact difference between a controlled explosion and a raw one. She didn't need to think. Every instinct she had was telling her to go, find the origin of this thing, find out who was doing it, and see if she could stop it. You'd do the same thing about the bomb, the gun. You'd do the same about any weapon.

She seized her red polyester robe and ran to the cathedral square. Even before she arrived at the end of the lane, she could see that the whole town was there, the students and the police and the firefighters with their narrow truck, but nobody seemed to be doing much. They were talking, some with their cafeteria voices on, some whispering and nibbling at words, some trying to get closer and others farther away. There was no panic, just a kind of hunger.

The tower's whole upper half, its delicate crunching medieval stonework, was ablaze with a sharp, hard fire that did not act like other fires. It was stable, like one of van Gogh's fires that looks like embroidery. Nonetheless, it was viciously hot and you could see the lead roof of the cathedral beginning to drip and weep, metallic tears from which parents held back their children. The molten lead looked cold and dirty. The flames, from below, were glassy; they moved too slowly, writhing, wry.

She saw the back of Torquil's neck and made her way over to him. He looked vague and faraway, and he took a long time to come back to himself. He said to her, "Beautiful, isn't it?"

She shook her head. "It reminds me of the problem in Marec's book."

"The Alexandrian Fire."

"Yes." Annae rubbed at her eyelids. "God. *Julius Caesar*

is burning the Library of Alexandria. He never meant to do it, but only to burn some things, some ships and old houses, things for which an emperor has no need. Now the scrolls are aflame, the walls are aflame, the men are aflame. People are carrying scrolls out of the burning building by the armful, and spreading them out in the road. What is the root of the fire? Is it in Julius's wars? His political interests? His family? Is the root of the fire in the tinder, the flint, the spark, the wood, or the mind of the man who set it? Imagine yourself standing amidst the scene, sparks flying up to heaven. How do you find the root of the fire? From what did it grow?"

"You've got every word," said Torquil admiringly.

"I didn't so much read that book as live in it," said Annae. "It was part of my English education."

"Mine too," said Torquil glumly. "That's how they get you. Well, I can no more find the root of this than the root of—of a carrot. It's *all* root."

"How do you mean?"

"I'm reaching out for the inside of it," he said. "I can get the wood—the wooden stairs, decorations, everything, inside of the tower, it's hundreds of years old but it's still got cells. I feel it—there, do you see them?" He nodded to where the firefighters' hoses had begun crossing into the flames. "Cool whoosh. Too late to save it. The wood's not telling me anything. The smoke it's become, it's not telling me anything. The fire didn't start in any part of the tower. It started in all of it, or none of it. There was no first strike."

She listened to him with the creeping fondness that often came over her with the people whose minds she read. When you read people, you got a *sense* of them— their pith and gestalt. The silty condensation of the personality, like something crushed small by the pressure of the deep ocean. You realized how individual they were, the way each unit of humanity is different from all the others, because it has been crystallized by the water or the atmosphere or the heat into a deformation nobody else shares. The fondness had nothing to do with liking or with loving. Instead it was the fondness, more or less, of a person for a pet, something small and simple in the home. It made her feel evil to feel it, and sometimes she liked that. Feeling like a villain, just for a moment, made her feel large and coherent.

She stroked the fire with her mind, looking for its root, replaying the exercise just as she'd learned it from the book, at eight and ten and twelve years old, a book that had always grown with her. It wasn't a book that taught you magic, exactly; it was a book that taught you to think like a magician, to become all mind, all air, to float above your circumstances on a cloud of thought and feeling. *The root of the fire.* Magicians think about system, symptom. And this fire, she thought, was a symptom of a magician who had lost control of his mind's ability to affect the world—it might have been anyone; it might have been her. Her vision expanded, a delicate gas swirling in the clear clean night air.

And then it happened, the grandeur of knowing something. A feeling like a building with a million floors, a million blocks wide, prismatic windows and inconceivable arches and a terrible weight that collapsed the caves below. She walked into the fire, heedless of Torquil's sounds of protest and his hand on her sleeve. She knew it would not harm her, as with an absent twitch of her mind she smoothed and protected her skin—the same instinct that made her rashes and marks now kept her safe and clean. She swept into the door like a queen in her red robe. Inside, the walls glowed with heat, the water from firefighters' hoses made a searing rain, and the truth was all around.

Annae-met-God. Annae-with-God. Annae-golden-in-the-tower. Annae-reaching-up. Annae-probing. Annae-un-burnt. Annae-up-the-stairs. Annae-in-the-flames. Annae-unburnt-again. Annae-tasting-the-flames. Annae-with-the-man. The-man-with-flaming-hair. The-man-reaching-down. The-man-troubled. The-man-vanishing. Annae-down-the-stairs. Fire cascading like molten fluid, concentration lost, she burst out the door of the tower with her red robe melting around her, her head, face, body, skin, hair untouched, and all unseen in her suit of dripping polymers.

Her mood of effulgent calm was departing; gagging on smoke, catching the panic of the fleeing crowd, she ran with them through the square and into the woods that bordered it. The woods were thick, and Torquil was very close before she realized the great noise of breaking branches was the sound of him stumbling over to her. When he saw the melted polyester ruins of the robe, he yanked off his coat and held it out to her, eyes averted. She put it on—shove of cold lining and scratchy wool—and they heard the patter of feet all around and the agonized creak and crack of the tower collapsing.

The colors of the fire screamed, drenched in carbon. Even the brown of Torquil's suit was saturated, seemed alive as soil. Annae felt that her heartbeat was faster than a living person's should be, and it held steady, not quickening or slowing. There was no place for embarrassment at being seen this way, only a kind of terror that was half awe. That feeling of meeting a god—it made no sense, Annae had lost her faith as a small child—and yet it had crushed her against it, it had been a holy dread, like something out of Coleridge.

It was then that Marec stepped out of the woods a few feet from them, and overwhelmed with the recognition that the man-with-flaming-hair had somehow been *him,* she flung herself into his mind without even thinking, knowing that the answer must be here—

~

Marec had been shown his age and it clung like hot phlegm to his throat. Marec knew he was not young; he possessed a mirror, and he didn't know why he had to be reminded of the obvious each day, stupid, stupid! Oh, he remembered when his mind had incised anything it encountered, when it had been a finely tempered needle, mechanical and smooth like those atrocious robots that his office neighbor built, with their skins of silken foil. His mind had been so perfectly at home in the stream of magic—his mind had been able to find better metaphors than "the stream of magic"—his mind hadn't needed metaphors because it was in magic all the time. It was Ariel who took it from him, Ariel who had been brought in to preserve him, Ariel who had departed with that particular color and sun and shade and afternoonity around his neck like a scarf that caught the black crisp weather in it, so that when you unwound it from Ariel's beloved neck you could feel Marec's heat and Marec's cold air trapped in the felted wool. Ariel had taken the sense of everything. He had taken all that was hard and honed in Marec, and made everything soft, diffuse. Even now he kept Marec's essence damp and beating, and if Marec could only reach in and take it out of him again—

"Oh," he said, for he had seen Annae and Torquil, frozen there on the ground like a snapshot, those two attractive idiots. *Here his thoughts bifurcated:*

—*Yes, attractive.* Torquil had hard little cheekbones and a beaky nose, which shouldn't work on a man, but does work in certain men when they're serious enough and have firm mouths. That's how David Tennant's face works. Annae's mouth was too generous for lipstick ever to turn it into a rubber band. Her eyes were big and wet, and her hair was big and dry. Even covered in soot and ashes, she looked famous.

—*Yes, idiots.* Annae terribly young and convinced her heartbreak was the first heartbreak on earth, Torquil none too young but somehow untouched by real sorrow. Torquil could be satisfied by imagined sorrows alone.

He wanted to please them and he wanted to hurt them, a not unusual combination for Marec. But watching them helpless there, he didn't have the energy to please or the heart to hurt them at all. They just stood there, looking frightened and sad, their faces slackening down. Annae had Torquil's coat on and he had his scared rubbery arm half on her, his flat hand pressed to her shoulder, his eyes alight and dead. Marec bit the inside of his cheek, hard, with intent. He stared at them sternly. Simple pity took over; Marec was capable of pity, dammit. He said, "Oh, Jesus, my place is up the way. Let me help you."

Annae was gagging on Marec's mind all the way up the hill. The thrill of the tower was gone, and she put one foot in front of the other, telling herself with every footfall that *this* was what happened when you allowed yourself to feel brilliant, *this* was the cost of knowledge. It was the dissection of your body. It was being taken apart feature by quivering feature. Not for the first time, Annae thought of the phrase "the curse of youth and beauty." Much though she longed to disappear without dying, her face alone would never let her. Annae knew she was beautiful, for she wasn't a fool, and she knew people thought her a fool, for she knew she was beautiful. She spat out ashy phlegm and thought grimly of her triumphant walk from the tower, just five minutes ago, her body radiantly unhurt, invisible behind the fleeing crowd, as much her own body as it had ever been.

When they came to Marec's house, Torquil said in a voice like a sob, "It looks like her!"

He was right; the house did look like Annae. The thick thatch mocked her bangs, and there were two wide blank windows with bloodshot panes, a pursed little door. To walk inside that mouth made her feel ill, but she was suddenly very tired and very aware of the dried bits of melted polyester sloughing from under the coat, and for the moment all she could think to do was sit down.

There was a half-eaten chicken leg on a tin plate on

the table, and a glass of wine, and a skin- and fat-speckled knife and fork that had stopped being used and started merely being dirty sometime in Marec's absence. Of all the state changes in nature, Annae was perhaps the most familiar with the transition from used to dirty. She didn't have long to contemplate this still life, for Marec put his stiff fingers against the small of her back, propelled her toward the dimly glimpsed bathroom, and said, "Go and wash up."

"I'm fine," she said. "I'd like to leave?"

"You're filthy. I'm not putting you in my car."

Floaters in her vision, soft sparks at the corners of her eyes. His voice sounded far away. She closed herself in the bathroom and sat on the toilet, her face in her hands. What was she doing in this program, this country, this house? Why did she not create an Ariel of her own—eliminate half of herself—split herself into two people and throw away the half that cared, as Marec had done? For that was what Ariel had been; that was the act for which Marec had become famous. The creation of another person from the scraps of himself.

She sighed and let her head droop. The forced intimacy of being in here, like being inside of someone's mouth. The room was disgusting—unventilated, plaster walls buckling with years of moisture, full of the clumsy evidence of DIY, the kind of work you'd expect of a man who knows his PhD qualifies him to be a plumber, a contractor, maybe even some lesser kind of doctor. Still, she got up, washed her face and arms in the sink, the grease and soot of the fire clinging to her; she tied back her hair by clutching it into a piece of foil she found in Torquil's coat pocket. After the God-meeting, the holy feeling, the flames of the tower washing down her back like hair or snow, the emptiness of this moment was plain and ugly. Her feet were sore and her skin broken, and she longed for the shawl knitted into the shape of DNA, for her computer and her mother's dog from America. When would there ever be rest and ease?

She dried her hands with Marec's hairy towel. Outside, the two men were sitting on the hearth, and their anxious faces pivoted to hers.

Marec said, "Oh, quit looking uncanny."

"I'm not trying to look uncanny."

"You—have—failed," said Marec, and handed her a glass of wine. It was his, smeared with bits of chicken at the edge, all too visible with the fire glaring through it. She looked at him, then understood: he had picked the wine up to finish it or put it away, but then been distracted, and forgotten, and had decided that it was a hospitable gesture. She put it down on the hearth.

"I can call a taxi," she said.

"You can't," said Torquil. "Your phone was burnt up."

"I didn't bring my phone. Can you—"

"Sure, sure," said Torquil. "Well, actually, I've never stopped using Uber—I know they're meant to be the morally bankrupt option, but I'm sure they're all as bad as one another."

He got up and patted himself down. Annae plunged her hand into the coat pocket; sure enough, there it was, but the battery was dead.

"Charger?"

"Mine's in the kitchen," said Marec. Torquil went to the kitchen, skimming over the brick floor in order to avoid the piles of trash Marec had left around. Annae and Marec were left staring at each other, then trying not to, and then Marec said in an odd voice drained of emotion: "You read too much, Annae."

"I got told that as a child too."

"Don't be smug with me. You know what I mean. You read too much of people's minds." Annae stared at him now with greater intent, with a shock that seemed to rake back her scalp and draw a spark from the end of each hair. "How would you know if I were doing that?"

"I can tell." He sighed. "Annae, I see myself in you. Or, more properly, I see you—in me."

"Fine," she said. "If you know, why do you think things like that about me?"

"Oh, I can't help what I think," he said. "Can you? But

we can help what we do, and I don't like what you do. You've seen me have private thoughts, painful thoughts, and now we are intimate in a way I *didn't* ask for and *don't* like. Please stop doing it."

"I'm sorry," said Annae, and she was sorry, now that they were just looking at each other and everything was ordinary. "You don't— I've had a rough time, Marec. Dr. Górski."

"We've all had a rough time," said Marec, and then Torquil was back, waving his phone in triumph, having called Richard in his Toyota Corolla.

But Richard drove aimlessly around town for ten help-less minutes and canceled, so Marec said he'd drop her off. Torquil followed them out, wrenched at the back door of Marec's rusted car as Marec removed things from the passenger seat—but then Marec gestured Annae into it, got in himself, and turned the key. Torquil was left jog-ging back, startle-faced, as they rumbled away. She gave an instinctive "Oh" of sympathy. Marec smiled tightly from his place beside her, and said, "I do enjoy making that man suffer."

The car wallowed through the black, pockmarked road, Marec turning on the headlights as an afterthought. She looked down at her hands, tucked in her lap and only slightly shaking. "What did Ariel look like?"

Marec sighed heavily, and she saw the wrinkles of his

face tighten. He didn't reply for a long time, and she thought he might bring up Jonathon's letter, but he still seemed shell-shocked, driven into himself as a blow drives into the skull. Finally he said, "He was ginger. Why was he ginger, I wonder? My hair was dark." He paused, for long enough that Annae worried again. Then he added, "He was young."

"Young?"

"Young, handsome. Well, I wasn't handsome. I made him— Do you know that I made him? You must know. You know his name . . ."

"Yes," she said.

"Well, you would. You were in love with one of my 'fans.'" The quotation marks were audible.

"I knew about it before I met him."

"And you know that I prefer it when people don't avoid the topic."

"I know that," she said. "But I don't like to avoid topics either. Only everything else."

He sighed again, and this time she smelled the sigh and realized that Marec was rather drunk. She slumped a little in the seat, with the vague sense that she ought to loosen her body, that it would do better in a crash that way.

"Ariel," said Marec, "was my better self. You know that? It usually turns out that way, I've learned. You know about Cedric Pickwoad?"

"No. Tell me."

"*Pick*woad was a late Victorian magician. He was at Brandford and then at Cambridge—at Trinity, I believe, or was it Trinity Hall? Back then it was easier to make the jump. At Cambridge he had a young, dynamic tutor. I say young and dynamic. He was old enough to have a grown daughter. Pickwoad was in love with the tutor. He wanted to be in love with the daughter. Do you catch me?"

Annae coughed, the smoke from the tower still rasping at her insides. "Yes."

Marec cranked down his window one inch. "It was 1897, and Oscar Wilde's trial was in very recent memory. Pickwoad was terrified of his feelings—of his *criminal* feelings. It took a strong man at that time to be unafraid. And so he took those feelings out of himself and made a homunculus out of them." Marec began to assume a more professorial tone. It sounded like something being dredged from deep within him. "Now, Pickwoad was unusual, in that most people make a homunculus out of their viler feelings. Or those that are merely base. As a result, most homunculi are dreadful people, or at least dull ones. I've corresponded with two of them, and you wouldn't take them as a plus-one to even a distant relative's wedding. Their creators gave them their fear or rage, and fear or rage is all they ever know. Pickwoad was different, which is why he reminds me so much of myself.

Most people don't have his kind of imagination. It takes an outcast to develop that."

"Have you been an outcast, Marec?"

She had been unable to disguise her dubiousness, and he blew air from irritated nostrils. "Perhaps not enough of one. Anyway, it was unusual for Pickwoad to make a homunculus, not from sin, not from vice, but from *love.*"

"Isn't love a vice?"

"How do you mean?"

"We want it even though it hurts us."

"*You* want it." Marec slowed the car's roll a little as it took the heavy curve into town. "Pickwoad's homunculus was made from his capacity to love men. Nothing else. But as I've learned to *my* cost, our capacity to love is what expands our thinking. In this case, the homunculus had all sorts of talents that Pickwoad never imagined. He could paint, he could sculpt, he was witty. He could seduce. Within weeks, he'd fled to the Continent with the tutor. Pickwoad married the girl, but he never did a stroke of good magic again, and I believe he ended his days teaching mathematics and magic at a grammar school. Meanwhile the homunculus and the tutor lived on in Paris, under the names Mercutio Taylor and J. S. Hall, and everyone who loves art knows those names, even if the name of Cedric Pickwoad is just a curiosity now."

He sucked his teeth, stopped for a little too long at a stop sign.

"I gave Ariel so much more than love," Marec added, a sharp whine at the edge of his voice like the whine of metal. "But I made him for the same reason. I wanted to be a better magician—free from distractions, of the flesh or the spirit. Stripped down right to the bone. That's why I gave him what was really fine in me. None of my fear or rage for him. Only the rarest cuts of Marec Górski. The best I had."

"The best?"

Marec was warming to his subject now. "Don't you usually find that it's the *best* of you that distracts from your work? Your moral doubts. Your maddening sense that as you get older, people get more complex. Confusion about what's right. Self-hatred, when you disappoint yourself. Knowing your limits. *God,* knowing your limits, the edges of what you're capable of seeing. As if a person can be a scientist after they've touched the edge of the universe and felt that it's only paint. When you get older, your imagination stops being limitless, and then that's it for your magic. That's the whole kit. Roll it up and go home."

"How much older?"

"Forty-two," said Marec without hesitation.

"Fifteen more years until I'm older."

"That's right, you've mentioned your age." Without braking, Marec reached out a skinny finger and dabbed at her cheek; she flinched from the coldness of his fingertip, felt that he was smearing the skin away. "What's this? A downy baby chick. You will learn all too soon of this complicated world, Anna. And you will *hate* it when you do, because your work will stop making sense. And maybe that's best, given what I'm about to tell you."

"You already told me—"

"I couldn't stop," snapped Marec; then his tone loosened. "I gave him what kindness I had, and what elegance of style. I gave him my love, though I couldn't bring myself to give him sex. I tried to give him my love of teaching, and certainly my fondness for the students, though there's muscle memory in the tongue and fingers still. And when I was done he was the perfect man. Christ, I was right to make him."

"And—what became of him?"

"He lives in London somewhere, doing social work. I believe he teaches yoga." They stopped under the bright fluorescent light of a kebab place, and she saw that a vein in Marec's head stood out pale against his red face. "Yoga!"

"If the perfect man teaches yoga, how can we say he's wrong?"

"I wasn't *trying* to perfect him. I was trying to perfect

myself. Jesus. The only thing that's fun anymore is telling this story."

"Did—did you give him fun too?"

"No, that just went with age. You learn to love everything or hate everything eventually." He came to her block and braked hard. "You live somewhere around here, don't you? All the Americans do."

"Yes, this is me."

"Well, anyway. How did we get on to the topic of Ariel?"

"I asked about him."

"Oh," said Marec, and there was a sudden fading in his voice, the volume being turned down. "Well, I just wanted you to know about him, because—because he's really a wretched man, and so am I. Better to learn it here than on the street. Get out, won't you? Which building is it?"

"I'm fine," she said. "I can walk from here."

"Good night, then."

~

At home, Annae took a long bath and went back to bed, thinking about Marec's mind. She remembered its smooth walls, startlingly like the Vietnam memorial, with words and names and facts engraved upon them and no way through. She had never seen walls like that inside somebody, and she wondered if they had something to do with Ariel. Most people's lost loved ones showed up in their minds like decay—like the last pile of blackened snow in spring, or the melted pop of a dead mushroom. Torquil's injuries had been all healed over, like lush patches in the grass where the mushroom had been.

She wondered what Marec dreamed about. Even at her best, Annae could never get into other people's dreams. The dreams were just hot glowing forms, gelatinous and soft, whose suggestive shapes might just be a coincidence.

Chapter 3

In the morning, things looked better. She bathed again and put on proper clothes—a long skirt and a soft, warm sweater that she dipped into like cream. The English autumn was in fiery blast outside. With the back of her neck still slick from the bath, she adjusted her sweater and went out.

The campus showered dry leaves on her. She walked past the Victorian buildings, which were designed to look like their Gothic forebears—dampened stone, unevenly cut, "bare" "ruined" "choirs"—along the sunny path of flags. Brandford was the subject of much snobbery, she knew, for being founded as late as 1836. Her seatmate on the plane over, a lady with a pink scarf and a thickly sprayed gray bob, had gently volunteered that "under all that masonry, the place is pure redbrick, you know." It was a term she had never heard before outside of a Le Carré novel. But to her, the college's eagerness to be thought old lent the place even more of a fairy-tale air. She was inside of someone's fantasy.

The wind was like her own calm breath. Strange how

this place already felt familiar, as if she had always been here. Even the flight had receded already, though she was still jet-lagged from it—all she remembered was legs burning with cramps, films instead of dreams. She'd arrived at an assigned apartment she had never seen, agreed to a shared lab she had never seen. All of it was just the same: a dream with real consequences.

~

The lab was a pleasant enough stone room, like a room in a castle, with two narrow windows, two benches, two sinks, and two chairs back-to-back. One bench—hers, she supposed—was bare apart from a ruined blastplate, cracked from end to end by some careless magic, on which she put her laptop. The other bench was crowded with plants growing in a soup of leaves and tendrils, their trays lit by white grow lamps, all atop an exceedingly scorched black stone blastplate with a cigarette stubbed out in the corner.

In the quiet of this cell (a monk's, a plant's, a prisoner's), she opened the laptop and let out an unconscious sigh, and for an hour spent her energy doing nothing but reviewing recent literature, immensely relieved to be researching again. She breathed in knowledge and breathed it out like dusty air. She weighed others' work, and for the moment did not weigh it against her own.

Then she heard sounds of people in the hall, distant footsteps, and then Marec's impatient voice. Her body jerked as if hit in a tender place.

"We need to talk about how you wash things in the break room sink."

"Oh, yes?" said Torquil's voice, high and feathery.

"You leave these hard lumps of *food*, Torquil. They're very difficult to remove."

"I don't know what to tell you. I scrub them with the sponge."

"This is the whole problem with you, my son. The motion is not enough, and you can see—visually—it's not enough—"

"Maybe we need steel wool."

"You need to use your fingernails."

"These food bits," said Torquil, "they're not even mine, and they've been in someone's *mouth*, Marec."

"So has your prick, and I guarantee you touch that."

There was a long drop of time as the footsteps halted just outside the door. Torquil's voice now was strained.

"I know you like your joke, Marec, but I'm a person. Not a punch line. "

"Don't underestimate yourself. One can be both."

Torquil threw the lab door open and shut it behind

him with one flap of his arm, damp-faced and red. For a moment she saw Marec's face, remote as a Rembrandt self-portrait, before the door replaced it. He looked like an actor, a little like John Hurt, although while Hurt's eyes could look sad or kind, Marec's were just organs. There was an afterimage of him in her brain, a smack of pallor and hair.

"How are *you*?" Torquil snapped at her, all leftover fury.

Annae shrank back and said, "I should go."

"*He* should go. You should stay." Torquil sat down at his own desk, stared at it for a moment, then briskly drew a set of microscope plates toward him. Little though she wanted to be in this room with Torquil's explosive tension, she didn't want to talk to Marec in the break room or the hall, so she sat down and looked nervously at Facebook, her concentration gone. Her mother had posted a meme with a picture of two hands just released from each other's grip, and the words "an unhappy child / hurts themselves / and blames the parent for what they've done."

Soon she felt the great heat of serious plant work—magic that produced heat so strong that the very foundation of plant work was to keep it from killing its subjects. She was very aware of the back of her own neck, wisps of hair touching the vulnerable spot. So strong was this vision that at first she was afraid she had read Torquil without meaning to, but then she realized she had only seen a lot of movies about vulnerable, fascinating women, made by men like him. She turned around, into the heat and light, and Torquil stilled his hands and kept them tight as broken things for a moment. Then he turned and opened a window.

"You have good hands for magic," she said.

"Skeleton hands," he said, and stretched them out appraisingly. He seemed pacified by his work. "I don't know if they're hands for magic, but they do make the gestures look good."

"I meant the skin. Your skin is very thin. It makes the force distribute evenly."

"Oh, right." He flexed them once more and went to stand by the whistle of air that came in through the window. "Sorry for the heat."

"That's all right. I'm sorry for Marec."

"You're a saint."

"Sorry *about* him, I mean."

"You didn't make him; he's not your homunculus. Or if he is, you've done a splendid job."

"He seemed keen to pretend yesterday didn't happen."

"We all do a lot of resetting here," said Torquil, jerking his eyebrow. "I've been to his place several times. He always seems to pretend it's my first. What are you working on?"

"Nothing. I mean I really haven't been able to do much lately. I came here to try to start again."

"Your rat fear remover? Hm. Punk band name."

She let the weak little joke disperse. "Hopefully. Well, it doesn't really remove fear. It just makes you care about it less."

"Oh. Like meditating, but very quickly."

"I hope so. Honestly, I've kind of lost the thread of that. It was early work, and when you show people an idea too much, it wears out fast."

"Oh, my God, you can say that again." Torquil reached under his desk, and she heard a plasticky tap; then he withdrew a pack of cigarettes that had been taped to the surface. "Mind? I have a spell for this."

"Okay."

He lit one, and the smoke curled into a perfect ball that expanded slightly but didn't spread. With a light, reassuring smile, he tapped it and it flew out the window, round and precise like a little balloon.

"Nice, right?"

"Yeah."

"I'm done with people who try to impress you with flames from the finger. What's that about?"

"I don't know. Men try to do that for me, and I don't even smoke."

"That doesn't surprise me at all," said Torquil.

Annae cleared her throat. "Well, what are *you* working on?"

Torquil blew smoke, tapped it, sent it away. "False cells."

"Really?"

"Yes, why?"

"It's like what a wizard would be studying on TV," she said. "Like a TV physicist says he's working on cold fusion. Or a TV mathematician says he's working on Fermat's Last Theorem."

"They solved that, you know."

"I'm aware. I haven't watched TV in a while."

"Oh. That's good! It's my main vice. Hours and hours until I fall asleep. Sometimes I don't know in the morning if what I remember is a show or a dream."

"I felt that way about the plane here," she said. For some reason her voice sat awkwardly in her chest, as if partly lodged there. "I was just thinking about that. We watched movies on the built-in screens. I was the only one who couldn't sleep. I must have done three or four whole movies."

"Yes, exactly." Torquil rocked a little on the balls of his feet. "But false cells aren't like cold fusion or—let's say the Hodge conjecture, that's a good one that's still unsolved. I can make a cell for you right now."

"Really?"

"Look. Here." He put out his cigarette and motioned her to the microscope he'd set up on his bench, shook out his wrists, took hold of a slide. "See?"

She peered at the slide, aware that when you look into a microscope you leave your body. You only see the light and the dark.

"Now look," said Torquil behind her, and then the heat of his breath merged into a larger heat, so intense that she had to close her eye; when she opened it through a watery haze, she saw the cell assemble—the thin honeycomb edges and the pudding in the middle, and then a slow wash of animated green.

"Chlorophyll," he said. "Easy as that. I can pull it right from a thought—make it out of any foolish little thought I'm not using. The challenge is one of scale. The effort, and of course the heat. I can heal a bone or make a sandwich, but the heat will fry your flesh, and the sandwich you definitely wouldn't like."

"Why haven't I heard about this, Torquil? This is— this is a huge advance. Even I know that, and I don't know anything about plant magic. I mean, it's— I've never seen anything like this."

"Marec blocks everything I write. Nothing gets out. I've been a year from finishing my dissertation for six years."

"Why?"

"He doesn't want me to publish until I've got it really sorted out." Torquil snorted and pinched his fingers around his long, delicate nose. "He says I'm prone to talking about a thing before I understand it. He's right."

"Or maybe you talk about a thing in order to understand it."

"Another American affectation. Here in the real place, we believe you can't learn without being almost continually told you're stupid."

"Thank God I'm too old now for *that* to stick."

"Are you? *I'm* not, and I'm fairly sure I'm older than you." His little eyes glittered at her, and his small mouth worked. Finally, the result was "I did Google you, you know. After."

"Did you?" she asked him coolly, assimilating the lie.

"Yes. I'm very sorry."

"Why?"

"I think it's wrong."

"Everybody does it," said Annae, a bland taste in her mouth, her heart heating up. How could she shame him, when she spent every night swimming through the dirty water of other people's minds? "Do you regret finding out anything in particular?"

"This person," said Torquil, and hesitancy came to his voice; he had been confident, even smug, when talking about his work, but now it had left him. "Jonathon. Was that article his idea?"

"I don't know. I've tried not to read it."

"Fine," said Torquil hastily. "I'm sorry. It's just that— I gather that he was your advisor. Or your supervisor in some other way."

"Jonathon? Yeah."

"He didn't seem like a good man."

Annae felt her mouth pull tight for a moment. "It's difficult to see from inside."

"Look," said Torquil, "you heard how Marec talks to me—I'm sort of glad you heard it, though I'm sorry you *had* to hear it. He's always like that. Everything is sex. He doesn't have actual intentions toward me, I don't think; he's straight and I'm ugly. But I know how bad things get when someone with power over you starts to bring sex into it at all. After I looked you up, I couldn't stop thinking about how easy it was for him to slip the knife between your ribs. And his career is probably fine."

"I guess I shouldn't pretend we weren't together."

"I'm sorry for guessing."

"Well, he has an endowed chair now," said Annae. They were sitting a little too close together on their lab stools, their knees just a foot apart; funny how you could feel so much safer reading a person, curled up inside their head as tight as a jarred specimen, than you could in proximity to their body. "Thanks for your sympathy, Torquil. I don't really like to talk about this with strangers."

"That's fine, of course," he said. "Naturally. I'm sorry. But I couldn't help talking about it. When you know more than you're supposed to about somebody, it's a sharp little thing that gets at your insides until it works its way out. That's why I try not to know anything."

Annae felt herself flush. She wanted to agree—to say, "Yes, it shames you, it makes you ashamed"—but instead she just said, in an overbright voice, "Do you? Manage not to know anything?"

"No." Torquil exhaled heavy air. "Did you know much about Marec before you came here?"

"I thought I did."

"Why do you say that?"

"Well," she said, "I mean, his reputation precedes him."

"As . . ."

"As the man who made Ariel. But somehow I thought he'd be a different kind of disaster."

"How so?"

"I thought he'd be charming. When you read the book or when you look at old video of him giving his lectures, he seems magnetic. That's not always good—you were right that Jonathon was magnetic too, which is great unless you're a credit card, or a hard drive, or another magnet who just had your own ideas about which way you wanted to be aligned."

"What makes people magnetic? As a man who has always been an inert lump of lead, I'd love to know."

"It's ego," said Annae immediately.

"People are attracted to people who seem strong?"

"People are attracted to people who seem weak."

"Then why isn't anybody ever attracted to me?"

"I don't know you and have no way of answering that, but I'm telling you, people are drawn to egoists because they seem *weak*. They seem so damn full of themselves that you don't need to worry that they'll swallow you too, and they're such *simple* people—you think you can manage them, can handle them, because you've got their number. Only pretty soon, you learn that once you've got theirs, they've got yours. And then you're taking calls every hour of the day or night. And then this isn't a metaphor anymore. You're really doing it, and you're thinking about them all the time."

"Right," said Torquil. "My God, you have a talent for this."

"I don't really," said Annae. "You should have known me in high school. But I've learned a lot about how people work since."

"So that's what you thought Marec would be?"

"Yes, but instead he's just sad and unpleasant. Is he always exactly like this?"

"I told you about the five British boys and the American girl," said Torquil glumly. "She always leaves after one year. He's not just unpleasant, he's—because of Ariel, he's actually a half person. You know how most people usually mix the bitter with the sweet, and often the worst people are the most charming. Like you said."

"Of course."

"I wish it followed that the least charming people were the best," he said, and this time she caught a tenderness in his eye, a faint quivering motion to his sensitive nose, that for the first time did not seem self-pitying. "Although— you're very charming, Annae, and I think you're also a rather good person."

"I'm—" Annae didn't know how to finish the sentence. She just said, "You don't know me. I'm actually a completely hateful person."

"I would like to judge that for myself," he said soberly.

"Well, keep working in the same room as me, and I'm sure you will."

"I get it," he said. "No, I really do. I get the hint, but—I can be your *ally,* Annae. That's what I want. I want you to last longer than the year. He always puts them with me, and I always watch them get hurt, and withdraw, and go."

"What happens to them?"

"Jennifer left," he said. "She quit the field entirely."

"Tell me more," said Annae, when it became apparent that he didn't want to go on.

Torquil took a long breath. "Well, it wasn't complicated. She wasn't very skilled or very serious. A dilettante, honestly—Marec can't attract world-class people anymore—but a nice woman. She did plant work too. She's the one who wrecked your blastplate. Jennifer had a great mind, but you could tell she'd been resting on that mind for years, and on her charm. Marec could tell too, and he called her out on it, repetitively, relentlessly, sometimes with the same words in every class. She would come out of his office crying—you have to meet with your tutor here every week, someone will send you an email about it soon—and come here, and tell me about it, right where you're sitting. He didn't even give her any notes, is the thing. He just said these things, which were true, so she couldn't argue. But he didn't give her any suggestions—any ideas for how to change them."

"That can be worse," said Annae. "When they have suggestions."

"Wasn't worse for Jennifer. Whoosh. Before Jennifer was Rashida, who's okay, actually—she's somewhere at Oxford now, doing pure math. The worst thing that happened to her is that she lost a year, because she was trying to decide whether to do pure math or this extraordinarily sophisticated renewable energy stuff that I don't even understand, transmuting nuclear waste into usable fuel with this time-travel business that somehow didn't rot your hands—I didn't understand it, I guarantee Marec didn't understand it, and he just gave up, just ignored her. Rashida didn't cry over it, not like Jennifer cried or Heather before her, but she withdrew, she never came to the lab, she went through some mental health stuff, she left, Oxford, bam. She'll be fine."

"And Heather?"

"Heather was his type," said Torquil delicately.

"Oh."

Torquil made a crumpled, distressed face. "He likes a certain kind of blonde. You don't have to worry about that."

"I see," said Annae, and looked down at her hands, then out the window, trying to recapture the autumn heat of the view, the softness of the morning, but the morning had blown off now, and left only a rattling of leaves.

"How about a coffee," said Torquil, sounding a little desperate to calm her down, although she was calm; he was thinking of himself. "Let's get out of here."

"Another time," she said, with the feeling that her voice was smothered in muscle, deep in her chest. She did leave though, and she had a coffee alone, staring into the hot cup whose handle burnt her hand.

~

When Torquil had told Annae about Jennifer, who had rested on charm, she had felt the most dreadful sense of recognition. Oh, she would never have said that she herself rested on charm, especially not now that years of pain had worn down her stamina. But once, she had studied the subject as if for a national exam. She had cultivated an air of whimsy until it was so much labor that she could barely think of anything else. In the years of her success, it had felt as if charm was resting on her.

Annae had once been a small, obviously autistic child who chewed her hair and avoided people's eyes and talked maniacally about whatever fascinated her most at the moment. She'd known no one liked her shrill voice, the keening sounds she made when she ran. She knew they didn't like how smart she knew she was. And so she had studied style, studied whimsy, studied poise. Style, because it was a shield; whimsy, because it was a sword; poise, because it was a suit of armor.

Of the three, she became best able to use whimsy. It was the only one of the three that struck her as an offensive weapon, something you could use to slash forward, something that would let you devote your life to thinking without fear of mockery. To be whimsical was to be wonderstruck, and wonder intimidated no one. On the contrary, everyone could look down on you for your naivete. And so with her science-themed knitting patterns, with her colorful dresses and narrow-waisted skirts and bright shoes, and with her straight brown hair and long brown bangs, she grew into an Annae who beamed wonder at everything and everybody. She had invented a translucent veil that allowed her to meet people's eyes.

Jonathon had crushed much of that out of her, not so much Jonathon the man as Jonathon the source of constant exhaustion. What remained—a pair of pajama pants with brains on them, a specific light and fluting laugh that came out when someone had embarrassed themselves, perfect physical control over her dimples— no longer made much sense, as a unit of charm. But nonetheless, the trappings and the muscle memory remained. And so she could see she was vulnerable to the charge of being a charming woman.

~

When Torquil had told her about Marec, she'd expected to suffer a similar fate to Jennifer's. She expected to be called out and complained about, especially given the pressurized environment of Marec's seminar, the faintly terrified and interchangeable young men. But what happened was the opposite: instead of high pressure, a depletion of the air.

For the first week, she experienced a jag of activity. Her pleasure in her work was hard to keep down entirely; it rose like a dry heat. She began to design a new animal study, to replicate her earlier work, this time with macaques. If she could make the work safer, this gentle laying-on of hands to the amygdala, if she could simply make it so that the fear and anxiety could slough off in the form of an innocent substance—if it could be transmuted rather than fleeing deeper into the brain and creating cancer—so many ifs, but at some moments the answer felt very close.

The danger was excess of zeal, of passion, even of compassion. If you make the amygdala too powerful, you get anxiety. If you shrink it, make it unresponsive, cut out the firing of the nerves, you get psychopathy. A silly over-simplification, of course, and one she had used too many times on student tour groups, but it would do. The goal was to delicately pull out some of the anxiety, as a bee-keeper pulls out a comb of honey, and replace it with something innocent, and balance the humors.

She prepared a long list of talking points about the study, and she waited outside Marec's office on the day they were first set to meet. The time came and went; he wasn't inside; he did not arrive. She pressed her head to the rough dry wood of the door and thought, well, surely this is an innocent mistake. He talked to me before, he was almost friendly—

~

After the second week of silence, with the sun burning low and casting shadows like scorch marks along the grass of the quad, she made her way back to her lab. She was going to talk to Torquil, or write a hapless polite email to Marec, a flurry of an email: *Dear Dr. Górski, I'm very sorry, but I haven't seen you in your office at our last two planned meeting times—do I have the time or place wrong? I don't want the term to start on the wrong foot.* When she opened her laptop in the empty lab, however, there was an email from Marec:

> *Anna, I have just seen that we were meant to meet this week and last in my office. I haven't got time to speak to you. Please sum up what you're working on in monthly reports, and we will see each other at the seminar meetings. Marec Górski.*

Hardly able to think, she wrote out a reply.

Dear Dr. Górski,

If you aren't able to work with me, can you possibly suggest a different tutor here on campus for me? Without regular mentoring, I know I will hit a wall with my research. I have been planning more advanced work than I've ever done before. I don't want to bother you or make undue demands on your time, but if one of your colleagues can take me on, I would be very grateful.

Annae Hofstader

A, he wrote back instantly. *If you are incapable of doing the sort of work we do at Brandford, I suggest you leave Brandford. If you require constant supervision to do your research, then I do consider you incapable of doing this sort of work. I have my own important work to do, and though we must jump through these hoops to keep the college rolling along, I'm under no obligation to do wiggles and tricks while I do it, and neither are any of my very busy colleagues. One piece of advice: Let go of this fear of yours. If you fear hitting a wall, you will never run fast enough to keep up. M.*

After that, she avoided him. She worked on more literature review, designed and redesigned her new study; she emailed it to him asking for approval, even approval under his name, but was always told that it "needed work," to "push it further," that "I don't have time to baby you along." The next seminar session came and went, and she was asked to stand, to give an accounting of her time. When she finished, Marec looked at her and said, as if sincerely puzzled, "You have wasted it."

"I've designed—"

"You keep talking about what you've designed, yes,

but what have you designed? Another version of the experiment that got you put on television."

"It'll prove replicability," she said. "I'm trying to take the next step up. It's good science. I'm doing the *opposite* of repeating myself—"

"You're saying that as if saying it makes it true," he said, with a droll little *V* of a smile.

"It is true," she said, knowing that her voice was growing higher. "If I were repeating myself, if I were just trying to get on TV again, I would do something big and flashy and risky. But—"

"Oh, sit down, Annae." He spoke as if they'd been sick of each other for years. She stood there, flushed and at a loss, until he snapped, "Sit *down!*"

She went home that night and wanted to split her skin open, wanted to step out of it, a creature of swirling light, and walk through the streets of Brandford blinding everyone who saw her. She thought of Jonathon, and how cool and peaceful his home had been, even in San Cipriano's summer heat. That smell, that *smell* of expensive organic cleaner like some cool grease exuded by pine trees if you knew where to look, like wet amber. And the neat bushes, and the way the sky lit up the windows as if plastered against them. Nostalgia corroded, she knew, but it was the only drug that could touch her today.

In this way, she got some distance into the term, the way you get some distance into the side of a hill when your car crashes into it: first things happen very quickly, but then it's hard to imagine progressing further.

Chapter 4

She was surprised to find that Ariel was easy to contact. He had a website; he was a therapist in London. He still used Marec's surname. She was even more surprised when he wrote back immediately to her email, offering to help her however he could. She'd elected to portray her problem as a professional one—needing advice about working with a difficult man whom Ariel knew well— rather than the more complex and paranoid-sounding fact that she also suspected he was the cause of the fire in Brandford. But it was apparent from the first moment that Ariel would have answered either question. He had suggested a café, just as if she had asked him for an informational interview. He had used three exclamation marks in five sentences.

When he waved her to his table, she thought that he looked like a man from an anime, one of the classy cyberpunk ones from the early 2000s where everyone has more or less realistic proportions. Long red hair, smooth and clean and so recently combed that the lines were still visible, like a Barbie head; a long, elegant nose; a smiling mouth, the wicked lips of a 1990s movie star. The whole of him put her in mind of a hologram, a lenticular picture, calculated to show you the progression of desires from your past (first the fancy Barbie, then the anime boy, then the real boy on the screen, and now—?).

Still, there was something about him essentially sterile, antibacterial. It was hard to imagine touching Ariel, though he was right there and showed every sign of humanity, a shed red hair looking dry and itchy on his tweed sleeve, a half inch of hairy shin on his crossed leg, a slightly tired and fumbled look. Not only was there that sense of seeing him on a screen or in an ad, but the essential *1990sness* of him felt like trying to touch a memory.

"You're the first of Marec's students who's ever asked me for help," he said now, taking a careful little sip of his plastic-topped coffee. They were in London, at a Starbucks across from the British Museum, and just outside there was a poster of the Sutton Hoo helmet with its air of sunglassed indifference. "Mm. Oh, this drink is awful. How's yours?"

"It's all right. It's coffee. It's the world's most perfectly average coffee."

"Is that why you like it?"

"Yes," she said, surprised at herself, and without her permission a gasping sigh came from her throat.

"Why is that?" He was looking at her with gentle curiosity.

"The, um. Sorry." She was dabbing at her eyes. "This is the first time anyone's asked me anything normal about myself in weeks."

"Anything normal?"

"Small talk. People in Brandford only ever make pretty large talk."

"Small talk is the most important talk," said Ariel, cupping his drink between his hands as if to warm either it or them. "It's when we tell people everything. What we think is polite to ask. What we think they might like to hear. By extension, what our family is like, and our town, and our country. I don't mean to load too much meaning onto what you think of Starbucks, of course. Small talk says more about the asker than the askee."

"What does yours mean?"

"That I don't want to talk about Marec," said Ariel. "But I will, if it will help."

"I'm sure you're very busy. I'm sorry."

"No, don't be. I do want to help. I'm made to help. Although, if I may say so—" He paused, searched for words. "First things first—are you safe? Are you all right?"

"No," she said, the word a chip of wood in her mouth. She had not expected her damp eyes; she had not expected to say no to that question. Life was so much simpler, and you surprised yourself less, when people didn't ask and didn't care. You could keep these things tamped down almost entirely if no one drew them out with their heat.

"Say more?"

"There was a fire," she said, and hesitantly she told him the story of the tower.

He listened with gratifying alarm—Annae had to admit that she never grew tired of explaining magic to non-magicians—and at length asked, "Why did you *do* that?"

"Spirit of inquiry."

"Were you sure you wouldn't burn? I'm—not a magician myself. At all."

"I was sure enough." She breathed in, felt cold air on one of her bad teeth—graduate student dental insurance—and closed her mouth.

"Really?" Ariel broke into a smile, looking impressed. "The spirit of inquiry alone?"

"It was bizarre. It was terrible." She stumbled over the words, unable to explain the real allure of the burning doorway, the desire to fling herself into something large and empty. "I wanted to know why. And in the flames, I saw your face. You say you're not a magician—"

"I'm not. Marec kept that. I don't even have any memories of performing magic."

"But then how did it happen?"

"Okay," said Ariel, and somehow the word came out as a breath, a hesitation, despite the hard *K* of it. "I've got a theory. Marec is—he's passive-aggressive."

"I'd say so."

"It's not a medical term, but it's useful. His anger comes out in other ways than speech."

"Are you sure about that? It seems to come out in speech a lot."

"Oh, there's more underneath," said Ariel. "I've never known it to be so extreme before, but sometimes, around him, things fall apart. That's just the way he is. He—" Ariel had gone pale. "I'm sorry, this is difficult for me to talk about. The time after I was born was very strange. Marec and I lived together. I stayed in his house; I had nowhere else to go and no money, and I was afraid of going out. He would often be very angry at me, and when he was angry, the house had bad luck, and so did I. The flame on the stove didn't take the gas, and there would be too much in the air. There would be sparks in the fireplace. Thatch would come off the roof. I remember most things about being him, before we were split apart. This didn't used to happen, or anyway Marec wasn't aware of it happening. After I was removed, that's when it started. Do you know if he was angry that day?"

"He's angry every day."

"Oh, you're right." Ariel slumped in his chair, his body a narrow tube. "That's all I can tell you. I suppose you saw my face because he was thinking of me. He always is. It frightens me."

He remained there for an extraordinarily long time. First Annae was placid, then alarmed, then worried that she ought to do something. Finally she touched his arm, and he jerked it away and immediately apologized.

"Hair trigger," he said, and straightened up. "I don't know why Marec's this way. I believe that it has to do with my being taken out. You probably shouldn't make a homunculus. You're not thinking of it, are you?"

He looked at her so sincerely that she realized he wasn't being rhetorical. "No."

"Only sometimes, I can see from people's look that they're—capable of it. Not that you would, or could, but you're capable. I'm sorry, I'm speaking in the full pomp of my ability to be honest, since you're not my client." He straightened up and gave a little humiliated smile. "Annae, can I ask you a bit about yourself, in return? I'm not used to speaking more than I listen; it's the reverse of how I talk to most people."

"You can," she said, through a flash and shiver of alarm. Ariel's warmth was real. She had not tried to read him, but she could recognize that from his ambience alone. But she was mindful that once, Marec had been a charismatic man, and she knew she was talking to the heir of that charisma, to a charm as sticky and sweet as a Jolly Rancher.

"Would you prefer I not?"

"No. I'm fine."

He gave a breath, a half breath, partway in. "Annae, I wasn't made to be very good at talking to people, only to love it, and so there's quite a bit that I miss. If I ask you a question, and you don't answer it honestly, I'll believe you. I was going to ask because I wonder how you're doing, alone in a new country with Marec."

"Oh," she said, and looked down at her dry hands, knotted together. "It's a lot."

"He's a lot."

"He told me you're a social worker?"

"Does Marec still think I'm a *social* worker?"

"Yes."

"I'm not. I'm a doctor of psychology. If he were more than Christmas-letter interested in anything I did—" Ariel seemed to choke a little on air. "That's why I talked about you not being my client. Though, to be honest, I thought you might want to talk to me about a personal matter. Not this fire."

"Why?"

"I don't know much about what Marec is these days," said Ariel. "But he tends to attract people with personal matters. They're the only ones he can get to stay around. Not that I'm better. But if you need a friend, I promise you I can be disinterested."

"It would actually be nice if a few more people were disinterested in me," said Annae. "All my life, people have been interested in me because I have a certain kind of face that I didn't ask for. All I want to do is bore people. I mean that."

"Oh—I meant *disinterested* in the sense that I don't have a dog in the race. But I suppose I'm not interested in you individually, just fascinated by people in general, and by you as one of them. Does that count as disinterested enough?"

She gave it real thought. "Why people in general?"

"Curiosity keeps me embarrassed. I need that." He coughed. "Forgive me. Recovering from something."

"You can get sick?"

"Certainly—in a sense, I *am* an illness, but it's a mental one. Starve a fever, feed an obsession. And eventually"— he indicated himself—"your obsession will find a form."

He was leaning toward her. The wavering of his body had a pleasing metronomic quality, slowly and softly back and forth. A heat seemed to radiate from him, like the heat that burned off when you did concentrated magic, bench magic, the kind that gently took focus from you for a few hours afterward and left you hallucinating lightly. She loved that, the gift of indifference that hard work brought.

~

At first she gave the biopic version of her life, the one she used for applications. She spoke of her childhood, of her favorite problem in *Twelve Theorems* (whose wonder, after all this time, was still not worn out)—

"Which one?"

"Number twelve," said Annae.

"The Ouroboros," said Ariel.

"You know it?"

"I know everything Marec's written. But I've forgotten quite a bit of it now, because it's not at all interesting to me."

"*The Ouroboros is devouring his tail,*" quoted Annae. "*He is a dry little snake and his tail tastes of rubber and salt. His eyes look sadly up at you. Nothing you can do can dissuade him from this course; it remains only to keep him comfortable. How do you begin?*"

"So you got through eleven of the *Twelve Theorems* before you really got interested. You were a child who finished books."

"Yeah. Well, the others were more interesting later. That was the one that fascinated me first."

"And how did you help the snake?"

"I kept trying to make him not want to do it."

"But I thought the puzzle says you can't persuade him to change his mind."

"I wouldn't be dissuading him. I just wanted to help him dissuade himself. There are lots of people you can't convince of anything unless they want to do it already."

"Everyone's like that, really," said Ariel, sitting back. "That's the only thing we learn in psychologist school."

"I was always proud of it," said Annae. "Ignoring the directions. I felt like I'd passed a special test. Like I was the only girl smart enough to see it: you don't have to believe what people say. I knew that if I disobeyed just right, I'd get a special stamp of approval from a hidden authority, just for me."

"Oh," said Ariel, and winced a little.

"I know."

"Marec and I were just like that." Ariel finally put his drink down and sat there looking at her with a face of blank distress. "It opens us up to all sorts of exploitation—not that the exploitation is your fault."

"You talk like every therapist."

"I'd be concerned if I didn't. You think it *is* your fault?"

"Yes. I know I'm not supposed to, but yes."

"Never mind what you're supposed to," said Ariel.

"Nobody ever benefited from trying to think what they were supposed to think. How do you feel about the people who used that fact to hurt you?"

"I don't know," said Annae, feeling a brief sideways lurch, as if she'd lost consciousness for a sixteenth of a second. "I mean, I really don't know."

~

Annae had met Jonathon in her first graduate seminar. This was in America, at San Cipriano, and she didn't have the DNA shawl yet, but she had had a scarf with diagrams of the twenty amino acids that appeared in the human genetic code. It was a simple Fair Isle pattern; she wasn't up yet to making lace.

The room was small and closed in, windowless, full of metal desks bolted to the ground and metal chairs bolted to the desks. The light in it reminded her of middle school, and that was cheering, for while middle school had been the worst part of her life so far, it had been the time she'd felt most alive in her mind. Every fresh layer torn off her brain back then had been a revelation.

She opened her computer, typed the date and the name of the seminar, and then he came in. Though the room was on the fourth floor, he seemed to blow in from outside: there was an outdoor motion in the soft heavy folds of his beautiful coat, and a few tiny leaves were scattered, quivering, in his hair. Physically he had a massive sort of handsomeness, and bright soft little eyes that settled on things easily. She got up to introduce herself and he said, "Call me Jonathon, do, please, you're in graduate school now."

"Well, if that's what you like."

"It *is* what I like." He smiled at her and turned to erase the mathematics seminar's notes on the whiteboard. "I can't believe they gave me this room. It is so— awful— for discussion!" With each word he scraped out a whole line of equations. "Even if the students talk to one another, they look at me. 'Dr. Bayer, I think Hubert's right about Pseudo-Geber.' 'Dr. Bayer, I think there are more things in heaven and earth than Horatio dreams of in his philosophy.' 'Dr. Bayer, I think Hornblower is blowing a line of bullshit right out his ass.'" The equations gone, he straightened his cuffs and walked to the lectern and smiled at her. "I've heard about your work."

"I don't know if you can even call it work yet," she said, but she was smiling back.

"I think you have the potential to be very good indeed."

"Thank you." The praise was his to offer, and she took

it. Then the other students began to come in, and she turned back to her computer, conscious of the thin clay of makeup applied over her blushing face.

~

At the end of that term, he asked to talk to her about her final paper. He had a tiny office, but with a nice midcentury desk and a wall so thick with books that the sour smell of old paper was squeezed out of it like juice. There was no ventilation, so he kept the window open and his plasticky tweed jacket on all the time. The window looked out onto a square of park, salted with cool water that kept it shiny and sleek. Generations of magic undergrads had done their first simple experiments on that lawn—plant growth, slow-time, fast-time, water devaporation. Because of this, you could walk on the lawn with shoes on, but it was dangerous to walk on it in sandals. As for lying down, someone or other would always open one of these big windows, like Jonathon's, and yell down at you not to do it.

"People like you are the future of our field," he was saying earnestly, pushing the paper back at her across his desk. ("Using Probles's Method to Enhance Serotonin Levels in the Rat.") "I don't think any of these numbskulls are doing anything like this, so conceptually deep. Half of them are still working on the damn lawn."

"Well, they're not interested in the same things as me."

"I don't know why it is that magicians in their early to midtwenties are all still completely hung up on botany. It's a *pretty* field, yes—touch a plant and watch it curl up—but it's all romance, no art."

"Oh," she said. "The A-word."

"Do you really think there's anything bad about it?" He was looking at her intently.

"I've just never *seen* it as an art."

"Ah, that's what everyone says." Now he leaned back in his leather office chair and smiled at her. His office was all cheap opulence, like his clothes. "Every magician sees what they do as an art, while braying everywhere that it's a science. Now, I don't blame you for buying in. It *is* difficult, and we have such a vested interest in not being artists—if that's what it is, we don't deserve the funding we get. But as it happens—no!"

He spun around in his chair and yelled out into the wet air: "Get off the lawn! Don't lie on it!" He watched for a moment, presumably as the student moved, and said, "Stupid, really. It reduces you to a *Simpsons* character. But they just want to *lie* on it, like people just want to lie in a snowbank when they're freezing to death."

"You develop a sixth sense after a while?"

"No," he said, and pointed past her; she looked around and up and saw an angled mirror on the ceiling that reflected the view from outside. "Science."

"Ah."

"Actually, Annae," he began, and then there was a subtle shift in his face—as if some faint line or seam had vanished into it. "I think your paper's really something special. Would you like to revise it together and look at publication?"

"Yes," she said. "Of course!"

~

"Which naturally led to sex," said Ariel primly.

"Of course it led to sex," said Annae, although she had flushed. Her coffee was gone, and she was fussing with the empty cup, removing the plastic cap and putting it back on again, one firm press, as her mother had always put the last piece of bread onto a sandwich. Ariel was looking at her with a soft wickedness, a smile that took Jonathon into account.

"What a pig."

"I should've known it," said Annae.

"If you'd known, you'd be just like me—not a human being." Ariel gave a soft cough. "People like that are only transparent when you look back. Like one-way mirrors."

"If he's a one-way mirror, what's on the other side of him?"

"Every single thing that led up to him. We don't see that until afterward either."

"You really are a therapist."

"I'm sorry. It's a habit."

~

Annae wore a light dress to her first real date with Jonathon. It had flowers on it so red that a hummingbird came and tapped one once with its beak. Jonathon had roared a laugh, a real roar, rough and leonine. They were well matched, she thought. They were on a similar level—she all too often saw young couples where the man was forceful, the woman tiny in his grasp, a fibrous little thing. She was much more than that, an equal— they were an equals *sign*, two lines of the same length that only meant something together. With his love, he made her feel as big as him, though inevitably a little less substantial, because at this size her molecules were a little more diffuse. They were sitting here on their first date and he had already said he loved her. For Annae, who had always been nervous about how you converted affect into love, this was a relief.

His teeth were so white and his jaw was so large.

Among graduate students and postdocs, permanently poor, those medieval signs of good health were sexy and kingly. Only a few isolated girls liked the off-brand faces of the British celebrities. She leaned forward, into him, wishing she could get inside him, into his skin, his soul. But there was no getting in; she had not yet learned the art of reading. That, she had picked up later, when she had resolved not to let anything like him happen again.

He asked her, "So what drove you to this, Annae? What made you want to work with people who have mental illness? Have you got any in your family?"

"No," said Annae. "I guess I just feel a lot of affinity for people who need help. I always have."

"Affinity, what does that mean?"

"It means feeling close to someone, as a kind of natural ally—"

"No," he'd said, and his face had lit into something gentle, as if he were cupping a bird in his hand. "No, that's not what I meant. Why do you have an affinity?"

"Well," she said, "I've always felt sort of as if my emotions were too much. As if they were the wrong ones. I empathize with people who also feel that way."

"That's lovely," said Jonathon. "That's a lovely sentiment. Do you want to feel less? Do you want *them* to feel less? Is that the idea?"

"I don't want anyone to have to feel anything that distresses them," said Annae earnestly. "That's all."

~

"This is *before* it led to sex," said Ariel, mock-peevishly.

"This is after."

"Oh. I'm sorry. That was tactless."

"If Marec kept the tact," said Annae, "that's no great loss. Tact is incredibly overrated."

"Do you still think no one ought to feel anything that brings them distress?"

"Not that they *ought* not. But they shouldn't *need* to."

"Feelings should be voluntary?"

"I know how it sounds," said Annae. "But, yes, as it happens. I do think that. My whole life I've felt too much. What has it gotten me?"

"By whose standards? His?"

Annae closed her eyes: Jonathon, telling her that she was spending too much time with friends who weren't on her intellectual level. Jonathon, telling her years later that she annoyed all of *his* friends with her sophomoric ideas, and she needed to either speak more intelligently or speak less. Jonathon, telling her patiently that he had no choice but to read all of her departmental emails before she sent them, to prevent her embarrassing herself.

It was like seeing stage magic, sleight of hand, being done in slow motion. She said, "I know I was stupid. If that's what you mean. I know any fucking idiot could have seen through him, but I didn't, okay, because I'm a special kind of naive and a special kind of . . . of . . ."

"I'm sorry," said Ariel. She opened her eyes and looked at him: his voice like a woody violin, his large eyes damp with apology. "This isn't helpful, I know. I shouldn't have asked you to revisit him. I shouldn't have tried to be cute and coy . . ."

"You hear about older professors who fuck their graduate students and suck them dry," said Annae slowly. "They bring them in to 'collaborate' and they steal their ideas. They tell them they're brilliant, and then, once they've moved in and have gotten used to not having to live like graduate students, they tell them they're stupid. They marry them, sometimes, in the worst cases."

"You do hear about such people," said Ariel cautiously.

"Well, Jonathon wasn't older. But he was precocious. He wore me out, and I lost my—I lost my train of thought. Do you ever do that? Just lose your train of thought, for years? We threw out all my books because he already had a copy of all of them, and it was a nicer copy. I stopped feeling like I could even talk, after a while; I just stammered, I mixed up words, I said words backward. He was that critical of everything I said. I came out here to start a new life—and now Marec's here, and I don't know how to help him."

"*Help* him? Help *him*?"

"I'm sorry. A slip. I don't know where it came from."

"Annae," said Ariel, in a voice so gentle that it was like artificial fur, sleek and cruelty-free and almost as warm as the real, raw, ragged thing. "Let's get out of here and walk by the river."

~

"So," he began. The sun had sunk a little lower, and the buildings around this part of the Thames had taken on a blue shadow, as around a well-penciled eye—London was made up for them. Tourist barges ran sleekly up and down the river. Ariel wore a coat of russet wool, and he had even given Annae his arm, a fatherly gesture that satisfied something of the craving for human touch, any touch, that she'd felt since her plane had landed in London. Her bangs were damp with perspiration, but she didn't dare take off the puffy jacket that cushioned Ariel's raw bones as he rested his arm in hers.

"This isn't your business, Annae," he said. "And I don't mean it to criticize you. This isn't your problem, this isn't your—your *story*. I shouldn't have even brought up Marec and our little psychodrama—"

"Well, between the two of us, someone had to bring up *something*."

"That's true."

"I wanted to know about Marec. To understand if he's a danger to me, and— How am I going to deal with him if I don't know about him?"

"You shouldn't have to. Did you really have to come all the way out here just to finish your degree?"

"I did. Do you think I would have, if I had the choice?"

"I don't know," said Ariel, and his mouth pursed for a moment into a flat, wet lump. "Obviously I don't know much about your side of the academy these days."

"It's a small world. And everyone in it is friends with Jonathon." Annae brushed her bangs from her eyes and looked out over the water. "And I wanted to come to England. I wanted it so bad. Americans feel this way about the UK. We feel like it's a fantasy place, where we will be safe, where we can be healed and maybe meet some interesting little creatures."

"Well, that's how empire works," said Ariel, and somehow he was glum, muddy, in just the right way to remove any sting from this. "It puts out this mythology that it's the only really safe thing. The myth's meant strictly for the rich and native-born—warm house, outsiders out— but sometimes people on the outside get caught by it too, by that sticky promise of safety. To me, England is poverty and inequality and xenophobia, displacement, a system of education that teaches only rich children to think and then blames poor children when they don't get into Oxford. A country with problems like any country. To the Anglophiles, it's Narnia."

"You're right," she said. "I don't really know anything about this place."

"And I don't really know anything about America. But we can learn, I think." He cleared his throat. "Anyway. I'm sorry. We've drifted far from the topic of Marec."

"It's okay."

"He's my fault, you know," he said, and tried a weak smile. "I blame myself for him. When he pulled me out of himself, the cap came off, and the bleed started. I was the cap. Or the scab, if you want, I'm not very good at metaphors."

Annae stopped walking and glanced up at Ariel's face—he was taller than Marec, and so much younger—and what she saw made her feel embarrassed to be holding his arm, because there was something ashamed and remote in his eyes, and what was her arm next to that?

"Annae," he added, "I see myself in you."

"Marec said the same thing."

"You want to disappear, and I know it because that's what I want too."

She looked at him and then let go of his arm, facing

him. "Why should *you* want that?"

He put his hands on her shoulders. "Don't do it. Don't become such a person." She pulled herself away from him, feeling trapped and claustrophobic even in his warm grip. "I'm sorry."

"Why do people always think that because somebody abused me, I'm going to become like him?"

"I'm a fool," said Ariel. "This is why I shouldn't be trying to be your therapist. I should—I must recommend someone; you can't go on like this."

"I've *had* therapists."

"I can give you a referral to someone quite good who'll work cheaply. You need someone to take care of you." He had let go of her, was patting his pockets, although she could see clearly that his phone was in one of them and he'd already checked it. Her hand slid into the slick silk lining and pulled out the smooth black phone, like a black natural crystal, and put it in his hand. They were just as cold as each other. Phone plus hand, smooth, cold, like tears, and yet she couldn't make tears, not now.

"I'm sending you the referral," he said, his voice faraway, and he typed with one thumb without breaking eye contact.

"All right," she said hastily, "all right, I promise I'll at least look the person up."

He put the phone away. "I don't mean that you shouldn't

become like Jonathon. No one thinks you're going to become like Jonathon. I mean not to become like Marec.
Don't make someone like me."

"I won't," she said, trying not to be impatient, trying
not to feel as if he were laying it on a little thick. "That's
the last thing I want to do. Life is hard enough with just
one of me."

~

"One more thing," he said softly, as they stood on the
platform at King's Cross. Some Harry Potter fans were
photographing one another and laughing wholeheart-
edly at the little place where you could pose with a cart
that went into a wall. He had bought her a pasty, all beef
and celery, very nice, but her body cried out for vitamins
and she felt sleepy by his side.

"What is it?"

"You read minds regularly, don't you?"

"Yes," she said, defeated; was there no one here who
couldn't tell?

He nodded. "I thought so. It was just a guess. Many of
my clients do, if they've got the capacity—it's endemic
for OCD sufferers particularly, they can't resist checking
things. Well—there's something I always tell them." He
aimed his eyes at her, dropped his hot palm to her shoul-

der. "I'm not here to tell you whether it's legal or moral. And I'm not here to judge you at all. But it's awfully bad for most of us. You may benefit in the short term from knowing what people really think of you, but what they think is generally dire, and wrong. You're breaking into people's houses to drink their poison. You can take care of yourself best by letting them shut up, Annae, all right?"

Her eyes filled with tears. She said, "Can I hug you?"

"I suppose so," he murmured, and she curled her arms around him, the pasty bag clutched in one hand to keep the grease off his coat. He didn't return the hug at all, but stood there as naturally and patiently as a large dog, accepting the ritual and giving his warmth without any sign of comfort or returned affection. Nonetheless, she felt calmed.

"I'm sorry to take up so much of your time," she said, aware that she was mostly just trying to make him feel better. "You've helped me."

"I do always try to," he stammered, and then the train began to pull in. As she turned to go, he said more strongly, "Annae, take care of yourself. My dear, I need you to do that."

~

She rode the train back to Brandford in a muzzy, sweaty state of mind. The snack cart went by and she bought some popcorn, on the vague idea that at least it had started out as a vegetable. Her mind was empty of thoughts, except the thought of Ariel's hand on her elbow as he'd put her on the train, and how sad and ashamed he'd looked. The referral was in her email, badly typed, and with the first name autocorrected into a noun—it said "Dr. Beyond Miller," a name which she wistfully Googled, hoping it was real. It wasn't, and she half typed a reply to Ariel before realizing she wouldn't call anyway. She curled her legs up beneath her, closed her eyes, and went into a half sleep, her lids barely closed over hot eyes, jostled open by every motion of the train.

Ought to leave. Ought to quit. No more magic, no more degree. But how could she face herself, if she did? And for what would she even have to live? She had put everything into this; she had lost everything else, sunk the costs until she was deep in the red. Most days Annae didn't even *want* to finish her degree. It was only the thing she was putting one foot in front of another toward. She didn't want to die, so she'd finish her degree.

She hadn't read Ariel once. It just hadn't been tempting; he had conveyed too much information with the cold veins of his own eyes, the wrinkling of his forehead. And she'd felt somehow that whatever was inside of him wouldn't be something she was ready for.

Chapter 5

The next morning was hard. She felt tired, more physically tired than she ought, and she asked herself, is this how it feels to get old? She sometimes felt so much older than she was—as if she had taken Jonathon's extra years from his shoulders, exchanged ages with him. Other people her age seemed too young and full of blood, flushed with the sensation of having time to figure things out, a whole bouquet of years before you were even thirty. Baby's breath. Looking back at the person she was trying to be when she'd met Jonathon—and had tried to be, increasingly painfully, when they were together—she felt she had nothing in common with her. All that wasted energy, spent on Modcloth dresses and vintage jewelry, on knitting and blocking complex lace.

She went to the lab, put down her bag. She was still doing endless literature review, familiarizing herself not only with the totality of her own field, but with neighboring fields as well, anything related to magic and the body. She fantasized sometimes about achieving complete control over her own body, manual management of the swell of the diaphragm, of the tingling synapses of the brain, the sluice of nutrients through the stomach and intestines. It would give her study results that needed no outside resources at all, and it would give her something to think about forever. Never again would her thoughts torment her—she would be too busy palpating her own heart, keeping a perfect rhythm like a drummer, regulating herself even in sleep, never for a moment letting a system spill away. Her therapists had always gone on about self-care. Well, she'd do that.

Behind her, Marec opened the door and said, "You've been to see him."

Annae's whole body jerked, and she groaned like a wooden ship sinking. Marec's dry hand gripped her shoulder. She said, "Get *off* me!"

"I am sure you are terribly triggered," said Marec. "How dare you reach him?"

She finally shook him off, heated and suddenly almost sick. "I can talk to whoever I like!"

"*Whom*ever," said Marec. "And I'm sure you can, but you may not. Haven't I warned you enough to stay out of my mind and my affairs?"

"I've stayed out of your mind. I talked to Ariel for *advice* about you." She turned on him, her voice cracking. "Did he tell you? Are you reading *me*?"

"Never mind how I know." Marec's face was red, a

smooth even color like a watercolor wash. "I don't go to your Jonathon for advice about you—in fact, I actively disregard what he says to me—"

"Why would you need advice about me? You refuse to deal with me, you refuse to talk to me, I'm trying to work without any support from you—"

"Because you've given me no proof that you can be trusted with the smallest thing—"

"You don't even know me! You just don't want to be bothered with me! You've thought I was a pain in the ass ever since you heard from Jonathon, a pain in the ass keeping you from working, doing whatever it is you do, because, what, you were so scared that I'd try to *fuck* you?"

"Because if he is telling the truth," said Marec, suddenly soft, "then you are not to be trusted, and if he is lying, then you have too much baggage ever to work undistracted, and certainly too much baggage not to distract me. You have no idea what I do because you have no *talent*." He broke off, strained his face toward the hall; footsteps were approaching. "You will leave Brandford," he added in a whisper, "sooner than later. I'll see to it. I had enough of you the day we met."

When he was gone, Torquil ventured in and put down his own bag.

"Was it bad?" he asked, high and feathery.

"I can't talk about it," said Annae. "I can't talk to you. I can't—"

Then the earth shook. It came as a single airy jolt at first, that moved them from their feet almost lightly. Annae watched glassware and books rise from her desk for a moment, as if by an elementary spell, pulling a quick G. Then she did the most elegant thing she had ever done. She took Torquil by his elbow and dove with him under her bench. He slipped beneath it, boneless, with less effort than any dancer. His body curled as he went, as dry and as open to the wind as something dehydrated, all cellulose and holes. Then the two of them were breathing hard as they listened to the boom and smash of the room destroying itself, and watched the lash of the tree as it thumped out of control against the window.

It seemed to last a long time. Annae thought of the way you're supposed to count the seconds between lightning and thunder, but there was nothing countable in this, only a wrenching and a dislocation and a collapsing of bodies into meat and wind. Annae screamed as a flask on Torquil's desk flew at them and shattered against her thighs, leaving sticky blood and a glossy residue of muscle and dust. Then the little room went dark, and she thought she had passed out, like in a movie: the camera still on, the darkness picked up with its sensitive eye. She felt Torquil trying to fumble out his phone, and then he dropped it with a snap. The room was now only the area under the desk, and from the offices around them there came a muffled screaming and sobbing.

She wasn't all right, but she could think. She had lived through earthquakes before, in San Cipriano, where there would also have been emergency supply backpacks on the floor under each desk, filled with seedcakes, whistles, warm blankets, and other objects of fantasy. Here there was only a quantity of dust thickened with hair, and the ooze of blood, and Torquil's rapid breathing. He was rigid with panic. She clutched him, trying to calm him, but her clutching only seemed to intensify the shock. The sounds around them seemed mostly sounds of pain. There was no speech in them at all. Annae reached out, looking for a mind to touch, but the narratives had broken down. Annae's mind, which vibrated and resonated under stress instead of merely shaking, reminded her that reading wasn't just about telepathy; it was mainly about seeing people's narratives. And nothing of that sort was possible right now—

~

Torquil's panic attack was becoming a solid wall of emotion. His body was one long scream. He could feel his mouth making what he'd read on medical blogs was called the O-sign, which means a person is close to dying (the Q-sign is for when they're really dying). Dyingdyingdying! the vibration coming in and out of him, half shaking his bones out of his body, pushing the sad bundle to the left. He couldn't feel his hands, and the sounds had gone. Only Annae's hot, damp hands on his shoulders were a constant; she was such a re-liable woman! But now the vibration was pulling him away from her too, and his hot, hoarse breathing was clouding up the whole space with puffy breaths of carbon monoxide, no, dioxide, trioxide, why not—

~

Annae was—

~

No, this was it, he was going to actually kill them both with a panic attack, a fucking panic attack was going to be the end of them, Pan with his little pipes sucking the air out of the room, sucking out Annae's sweet oxygen, sucking the very lin-ing loose from her lungs like the feeling of warm tendon on your mouth, a pre-vegetarian bowl of pho he'd eaten once in Glasgow with a girl he'd meant to treat but didn't, the red-and-green tinsel decorating the walls, although it was sum-mer, the grease on the tinsel dulling the sheen—

~

Annae needed—

~

Fuck it! Stop! *But when he tried to draw back his breaths, ease them with a firm grip back down his gullet like a really excellent pinball player aiming the silver ball, he could not; he could only pump them more, like he had his emergency reflexes just confused and something in him was trying to pump the brake pump the brake PUMP THE BRAKE— and then he felt better, he felt much better, and something wet and cold was dripping down the back of his neck.*

~

Annae took in a breath, the cold clay-mask stuff flowing down his neck and over her hand. Reflexively she brought it to her face, although she could see nothing, and smelled it, held it over her mouth to waft in its taste. A foot away it had smelled like nothing, but at this distance the scent of decay seemed to reach into her throat and make a trigger-click, a plastic button, bringing bile. She dropped her hand swiftly and wiped it off on Torquil's tweedy shoulder.

"Am I all right?" he asked her, his voice just right—not flat or remote or ragged with frayed energy, but calm, a little hoarse. No longer was the sheer force of his emotion pulling her mind to his. No longer was every second with him like the horrific intrusive thought that always came to her mind when she thought of the phrase "nose to the grindstone." Her mouth twitched, for she knew she had done something, done it instinctively, and solely to push his horror away from her, and Annae did not trust her instincts, nor trust them anyway to be morally right.

"*Are* you?" Her own heart was going off like a sewing machine with the pedal stamped straight down to the floor. "I took—some of your anxiety out."

"Do I have cancer? Like the rats?" In his voice now, a faint amusement.

"No."

"Well, at least you're sure of something."

"No," she said. "Doing this in rats—I could never get the emotion out of their skulls, just out of their brains. That's why the cancer. I'm oversimplifying, of course."

"Of course." Torquil coughed, then hacked, and she felt him shift in the little space. "It seems to be coming up from my lungs now."

"Better out than in. I really am sorry." It was starting to hit her, what she'd done, and she moved away from him as much as she could and compressed her hip against the wall.

"What for?"

"That's an experimental procedure. It's old, I haven't even done it in a long time, it didn't really work then, I didn't get your consent, it was against absolutely every man-made rule that I'm aware of. You could prosecute me, you could sue. That's only the beginning of what you could do."

"I'm not litigious," he said, and although he had waited a breath past the end of her sentence, his voice sounded as if he were interrupting her. It was the disconnect in mood that did it. He was very, very calm. Cautiously she touched her fingers to his pulse, felt it bumping softly, like an interested man going "hm, hm." His skin was warm and slick with the decaying fluid, and felt malleable as potter's clay under her fingers.

"Did you hear me?" he added. "I said I don't want to sue you. I haven't felt this good in—I don't think I ever have. And I'm under a collapsed building, running out of air. Oh—but hold on."

Suddenly the room was full of hot, foul air, a gorgeous gust of oxygen like a breath inflating a paper bag until it popped. She struggled to breathe it; it seemed denser than other air, but then by staying tense she managed to take in just a bit, carefully, and then it was all right. Her ears popped too, and her lungs felt like they might. She felt something against her face—leaves—a choking bulk of very hot and dry leaves, with serrated edges. Torquil handed something to her, a massive ball of roots that burrowed into the hollow of her hands as if shy.

"This'll give us oxygen," he said. "I made it out of some of the guck. Just like that."

"Torquil." She took, or gave, another deep breath—it felt like she was giving it. The burning air came more easily into her lungs now. The initial feeling that there were pinprick holes in them was gone. "It's awfully hot."

"Well." She felt him stretch out on the floor, heard his head connect with the dusty old wood. The sounds of agony had grown fainter around them, like the signals from stars. "Bugger all this for a lark. *My* God. Can you imagine what he's done to us now? Do you think he'll keep doing this to us until we're all dead? It's *No Exit* up here, but without the lesbian. I don't think I can stop talking, Annae, just as a data point. Do you realize what he's done to us all? I hardly knew it myself until this bloody moment."

"No."

Torquil took a hot breath in, an experimental cough, and in the cough she heard a subvocal jabber, half obscenities and half tears. "Every year that I've been here—and there have been seven, like sons, brides, and brothers—every year, something dreadful has happened. This one is bigger than anything I've known. The first year it was a flood in the town, one that got into the sewers and made them overflow. Nobody drowned, but people got sick, and Gordon—another of the grad students, I don't know why you'd remember him—had his basement flat fill up with liquid sewage. The second year it was a fire in my lab which set me back practically to the first year. The third year, which was like my second year, if you're keeping track of this conceit, one of our cohort died in a bicycle accident—went off a bridge, bizarre thing, a mad windstorm blew up, mad, right? My fourth year it was Maxwell, a *former* student, going through his windshield because all the dogs went mad and started running in the streets, and Maxwell, you see, loved dogs and was trying to avoid them. My fifth year nothing bad happened to the graduate students at all, but there was a fire in the president's office. Marec seems to incline to fires. I can't imagine how the tower managed to offend him, but then Marec *is* an architectural hobbyist."

"And last year?"

"Nothing. Waiting for the shoe to drop. And this year, two things. Making up for it." Torquil coughed, then hacked, more bits of words coming out in the rasp of his throat. "Annae. We must kill him."

"What are you talking about?"

"You know what I'm talking about."

"I don't." And the thought sprayed her brain with a

rich dust: *Oh, my dear God.* The total calm, the arrogance suddenly undisguised, the absence of regret. The amygdala. An oversimplified explanation. A true explanation. Too much activity there: anxiety. Too little: psychopathy. In her panic, in reaching into him and pulling out his ceaseless fear, she had taken his conscience with it. A man's whole conscience, half of his personality. What in God's name had she done?

He was still talking. "I know I'm way ahead of you on this. I am going to have to manage this project, but seriously, we must kill him. We must. And if we must kill him, we may also need to kill the ginger djinn. If he doesn't simply die with him. Does he? Look it up."

"Why? *How?*"

"Your mobile *tele*phone. You still have it in your pocket."

Annae reached into her pocket and took out, yes, the phone. She turned on the flashlight, making shadows that turned around the fallen rubble, the massive leaves of the breathing plant that covered most of their bodies, Torquil's upraised knees, his fallen face turned partly to look at her, his stiff mouth somehow much more elegant than it had been. His hands lay disregarded across his chest. He said, "Do you know I've just realized *why* Ariel is a ginger?"

She flicked off the flashlight. She felt momentarily

helpless to use the phone, to call for help or otherwise.
"Why?"

"*The Little Mermaid* is all. He's seen *The Little Mermaid*,
by *the* Walt Disney Company. See, he wanted to name
him Ariel as an allusion to Shakespeare. But unfortunately, Marec is a plebian like the rest of us, and what he
really thinks of is that song, *oh-oh-oh, oh-oh-oh—*"

"Shut up!" came a sudden voice from far away. "Oh,
God, shut up with that singing. My God, my God!"

There was a bar of service and Annae tried to call 999,
but there was no answer, just a flat dial tone laid across
the way. She tried the only person she knew in Britain
outside of Brandford—Ariel—but he didn't pick up. The
news didn't have coverage yet. Her mother—

"Look it up," said Torquil impatiently. "Look up
Pickwoad and his homunculus. Give me that." He took
the phone from her. After a moment, he said, "No, no,
Mercutio Taylor outlived Pickwoad by *dog's years.*"

Despite herself, Annae was interested. "Really?"

"Forty years."

"How did Pickwoad die?"

"Guess."

"Suicide."

"Guess again."

"Not suicide."

"Cancer. Young. Marec's not young. You know how to

give a person cancer, you *barely* avoided giving it to me—"

"Torquil, this isn't right. You aren't right. I've hurt you, these aren't things you'd say—"

"How do you know what I'd say? We've barely met each other."

"I've been in your mind."

"Get into it now," he said, "then. See where it takes you."

"No," she said, and the word was heavy and solid in the air. She had not expected herself to say it, and she took a deep breath. "I'd be breaking into your house to drink your poison."

"Do you know what's *poison*?" She felt him very close to her suddenly, and his closeness made her shrink back against the wall. She smelled the chemical on his breath. "This shit you took out of me. This—this cold, horrible stuff—it smells like death—what even is it?"

"It's your anxiety," she said, and her voice sounded flat and distant. "It's what your anxiety became, when I took it out of you. I didn't mean to take it out for good—I was just trying to calm you down—but I think that's what I've done."

"Oh," he said. His voice was just as flat, but much closer. "Oh. That's what you did?"

"I think so."

"Because," he said, "I can't feel fucking anything."

"I know."

"Put it back."

"I can't."

"What do you mean? I thought you could do any-thing—you're supposed to be this ultracompetent, ultra-kind, ultracaring person—what do you mean, there's shit you *can't do*—"

"I'm a normal person," said Annae desperately. "A nor-mal, ordinary person. I never told you I was any of those things. You decided all that for yourself."

"Shut up."

"Okay."

"What—really?"

"I don't have anything more to say," she said numbly. They sat there breathing heavily of the thickened air, and for a long time she heard Torquil weeping, or trying to weep. The tears became sobs, the sobs became coughs, the coughs became the sounds of a hack actor, trying to convey an emotion he has never known in himself. Then he was silent. Annae tried again to call 999, but this time there was no signal at all.

~

When he spoke next, he was calm again, and not pre-tending to be anything else. "Have you given any further thought to the question of killing Marec?"

"Jesus," she said, her voice breaking. "What does Marec matter right now? We're going to die. Kill him yourself if you want to kill him."

"How? Should I make him a sandwich? You could get rid of him deniably, Annae. He generally selects his students for their offensive incapability. I mean, I'm a plant guy. But *he's* killing people."

"Does he know that?"

"Does it matter? *His mood affects everything about this unlucky town.* Why did your fucking Uber driver get lost in his own city? So Marec could drive you home and tell you about why he's innocent and the whole rest of the world is guilty."

"And because the tower was on fire."

Torquil sighed. She heard him sitting back. "My God. I really am sorry. I don't know what's got into me."

"Let's be quiet for a while," she said, "and wait for someone to help."

They lay there in the dark for a very long time. The cries around them bent, lost coherence, fled. Torquil gave a little gasp at one point—a rich sound after so much silence, full of details she otherwise wouldn't have heard—and said, "I apologize for this. Maybe we can make it into something." Then the splash and the sweaty smell of urine in the corner, which collected and soaked into the floor and filled her head with ammonia. No one was coming.

~

"Annae."

She woke up, black to more black. Torquil's voice sounded heavy and muzzy, far away. He said, "I've made water."

"I know, I heard you."

"I mean I've created clean water. For you."

It was very close now, and very hot. The oxygen plant was working, she could feel and smell it, but the air was thick with their bodies, with particles of sweat and stink that made them fill up the whole place. Their bodies were shaped like the room and the room was shaped like their bodies. Silence and dark everywhere.

"I've got it in my hand."

"You made it out of the piss?"

"Yeah. I had some and you should have some." His voice caught, dragged. "I'm feeling for you in the dark. I'm going to—" His hand connected with her shoulder, still in the good warm sweater with just enough silk dragged through it to make it soft, silk from India, cotton from Uzbekistan, polyester from midcentury molecules, assembled in Vietnam. Grave clothes, they'd survive her.

She felt his hot hand rub against the hot sweater, a very careful brush, just enough contact to help him find her hand, and then it came to her lips and despite herself she was opening her mouth, drinking. The water was clean and cold and unbearably pure, fairy-tale water from a fairy-tale stream. The making of it must have cost him three degrees of heat in this room. When she finished she pulled off her sweater and felt better. Who was here to see her?

"Are you taking your top off?"

"Yes."

"Give it here. I can get a little more water out of the sweat."

"This is disgusting."

"It's probably good for us. Exposure therapy."

"I've been exposed to enough in my life." She lay down on her side, aware of how petulant this sounded, but really, who would shame her for complaining here? Not even her mother. "Wait a little bit before you do the water, okay? It's unbearable in here already. And the hotter it gets, the more we'll sweat out."

"I know. Do you suppose people don't know there's anyone alive in here?"

"I don't know *what's* going on. Oh, Jesus."

"What?"

"I have a way to get a message out to Marec," she said.

"You can't ask what it is. It's something he's told me never to do."

"I don't give a shit what it is," he said, and then, with a faint horror as if he had touched something sticky, "I really don't."

"Hold on. Hush."

She cast her mind out, looked for Marec. All around them were dying people, their emotions a static scream, but she found him at last somewhere outside the building, and she plunged into his mind, trying to be as visible as possible.

~

And here was Marec, and Annae was with him.

"Get out," he said aloud, "get out!" The house was quiet and dark, its electricity shut down, all the light pollution of the campus gone and the stars very bright. He had a fire in the fireplace and was sitting in its flickering light, feeling like the last man on Earth—get out, get out!—his eye twitching, his back aching. When he'd been a young man, he had regarded older men's backaches with a certain coziness—the proud pain after life's workout. Now he knew what pain was. It was a tree of needles that grew at the base of his spine. Its branches stabbed his shoulders, and its roots ran to the ankle. When you hit fifty, this tree of pain was nailed to you, and

each day you were made less wise by the process. If not the back, it was the head; if not the head, it was the knees or the ankles. If not the ankles, it was Ariel's absence, like something removed from the channels of his bones.

Get out!

But he was safe here. Annae could reach into him all she wanted, though God knew why she wanted to. He was safe from storms, safe from earthquakes, safe from prosecution. He need not fear the consequences of what he did not mean, and God knew he never meant these small disasters; they did not reflect the core of him. His house stood always on the hill, never fell apart in the earthquakes, never gave in the storm. Poorly built though it was, badly thatched, with a fringe of girl-hair, it stood straight and earnest and looked out over the town with a judgmental eye.

Outside, now, half the college was gone. Little emergency vehicles rolling into town, all light in the dark, tanks from the army, perhaps even Prince William—or, no, it was Harry, whichever of them flew the helicopter. Whichever one still lived in the country. It was a dark, wet night, and the tanks and the fire engine and the helicopter all had to roll through the sodden crunch of rain on old leaves.

His vodka tonic was very strong. He needed it, though some days he wished he'd accepted his doctor's offer of Xanax, which struck him as cleaner and simpler, a shadow on marble where alcohol was a whole wasted muddy afternoon among the darker shadows of trees. Marec was alcohol; Ariel was Xanax. Two. Three. A bezoar. Irritably he raised the cup to his lips again and felt them cold and wet against the cold-wet inside. Ariel is a bezoar of twenty-nine Xanax.

He went back inside to his work. He was working in long-hand on a sheet of beige paper. Marec had always hated the texture of blackboard and chalk; he did not know how others stood it. Paper was just as impermanent, if you burnt it, and didn't involve grinding together rocks of different colors. With quick slashes, he cleft strings of flesh from bones—this paper was meant to be a new theory of homunculus-making, something that would prevent others from making the mistakes he'd made with Ariel. A gentler approach. More subtle gradations of feeling, to shade the distance between your personality and the new one, rather than marking it out with harsh, sharp lines. He intended to demonstrate that through sufficient will—

GET OUT—

Abruptly, the words were gone. One moment he was thinking, sufficient will, and then it might as well have been a reference in Shakespeare, "Whoever hath her wish, thou hast thy Will." He sat back from the papers as if they had physically repelled him, and breathed in air lit by the fire, and curled his yellow fingers in their sausage casings of clean skin. What was this? A crunching in the brain; a sensation he could no longer name. A tingle or a jar. A washing, a lightness, a wood. His head had swum—yes, he got as far as the cliché, but no further, and he could find nothing more accurate. He had expected it to be temporary, as one's little neurological twitches were, but it went on and on. He felt as if inside him were a piano pedal, and someone was pressing down on that hard, rounded lump of metal, polished by many feet—making everything reverberate inside him. The feeling was, the longer it went on, not unpleasant. Many things were vibrated use. Loose.—GET OUT, YOU'VE DONE THIS TO ME, I KNOW YOU HAVE—YOU ARE THE ONE WHO HAS DONE THIS TO ME—ANNAE HOFSTADER, HOWEVER MANY ANNAS YOU MAY BE—OUT—OUT—OUT!

He got up and rushed, unsteadily, to the window, to look out at the night. Wet here, wet everywhere, but how beautiful the clouds in front of the moon! How feather-light, how gray-dated by layers of grade, how impossible for an artist to replicate. And wasn't it a miracle, that window glass made it possible to look up at storm clouds without the drops hitting your eyes and making you blink. How strange, the ingenuity of people, which was nearly all focused on removing inconvenience. GET OUT—OUT—OUT—

～

Annae and Torquil were dug out hours later, after Annae, waking from her stupor to hear barking dogs nearby, played "In the Aeroplane Over the Sea" on her phone speaker because she could no longer speak loudly enough to shout for help. Torquil gave an all-over start when he heard it; she felt his shoulder jerk in the dark, now the exact temperature of their bodies, the plant rich on their flesh like kudzu. They emerged into the night, and in the stretcher on the way to the field hospital, she looked up into black glass and listened to a wet, balmy wind like something from Hawaii. They put her to bed and the last thing she thought was that it was good that it was night, she wouldn't be jet-lagged.

Chapter 6

Annae as a child had interrupted people all the time, because what she was saying was always the most interesting thing she could imagine in that moment. The words spilled from her, rags of ink and paper suspended in slippery oil. Once, at the age of five or six, she and her mother had been at the hospital, waiting to hear the results of an operation on her grandmother. Annae had been babbling to her mother about an exotic chicken she'd seen in an urban coop on the way to the hospital, and then a doctor had come in to tell her mother with great tact that the operation had failed, and Annae's grandmother had died. After what she thought was a respectful interval, Annae had returned to the subject of the chicken's red comb, and had been spanked for it. Her mother had been estranged from her grandmother; it wasn't as if the news meant anything to Annae, not as much as seeing a bird with black-and-white feathers mottled like a composition book. Years later, Annae and Jonathon would spend a drunken night Googling and eventually find out that this chicken was called a

Dampierre, and that it was a French chicken, and this news made them feel that they had generated a lovely filmic memory.

What Brandford did after the quake was like that—not the drunken night, but the interruption. It just kept on talking, and its voice seemed to grow higher with excitement, its eyes to shine. Annae couldn't be angry, couldn't fault it, because she saw herself in the town, its eager distribution of bottled water, its rapid reopening of shops. Whether its eyes were bright with tears, or mania, or the passion of helping people, it didn't seem to matter—they were bright, and they shone in the dark. The town staggered along for a week like this, broken-legged, the eyes bright perhaps with infection, now that one thought of it.

In the interim, Annae was cleared to go back to her apartment, where she found every fragile thing broken, all food spoiled. She went straight to her bed, the foot of whose comforter was covered in broken glass, and lay in it staring at the ceiling, thinking of Torquil and Marec. The horror of what she had done to Torquil still had not expanded within her—it remained as a small pill. As for Marec, she still didn't know what she had or hadn't done to him, only that she could hardly live with it.

The winter weather had come on suddenly, and ice coated the campus, but when Marec approached her, he ran. She saw him coming from a long way away, a black figure running without heed for the wet and sweat, miraculously failing to slip, flailing in all the right ways. When he reached her, he said without shortness of breath, "I know what you did."

One look at his face, working like yarn or thread in skilled hands, and she stopped quite dead. His eyes were paler somehow, as if some polluted film had been pulled away from their irises, and the pupil of one was a little larger than the other.

He gave a staccato laugh, an innocent sound, and pointed at the smaller of the two. "You've done this to me. I know it. I know what you did to me. I know. It's all right." His features parted into a rich, wrinkled smile. "You've shown me something very important."

"What have I shown you?" she asked carefully, looking into only that one shrunken pupil, not daring to explore the larger and emptier one. Her face felt tight, like a rictus without the smile.

"You'll have to wait to see it yourself. If it could be explained, I wouldn't be grateful." He grasped her arm; his touch was soft as felt. "Come and have a drink with me."

"I can't."

"Why not?"

"I don't want to," she blurted. "I just don't want to, Marec. We're not friends."

"Annae, Annae, Annae," he said, and she couldn't tell if he was joking or just stuck on the word, coming out as it did with more tongue than usual. "How *is* it that you're so broken and yet such a bitch? How on earth did you come out this way? These are the questions I want to answer before I die."

When she said nothing, he added, "I'm really asking," with a flinty grimace, as if two of his teeth had dragged together painfully and struck a spark.

"What have I done?" she asked him, not knowing whether she was asking for clarification or begging for-giveness.

"*This,*" he hissed, and put his finger to his head, gun-fashion, like a man miming suicide. "Whatever's broken in here. Of course you fucking did. You're a specialist in giving rats cancer, aren't you?" His voice grew high and cold and singsong. "That's your fucking spec*ia*lty, isn't it?"

"I didn't!" she said, although with a cold slippage of the heart, she began to believe that she really had. She hadn't meant to hurt Torquil either, after all, and yet she had reached instinctively out and ruined him, the way you'd brush a strand of hair from someone's forehead. In Marec's mind after the earthquake, she had seen something like a dam bursting. Whether it was a stroke, a hemorrhage, she didn't know—she had been focused on his mind, not his brain, but it was obvious that that was the effect. She had *felt* the line jerk, the noose tighten. Who was to say that it wasn't her hand on the line, or her neck in the noose?

"I told you never to read my mind again. Isn't that supposed to be what young people think? Aren't they supposed to care about *consent*?"

"Marec, I'm sorry, I thought I was dying. I thought you'd know I was there and help me."

Marec stared at her. She did not know if he was reading her, if he still could. His mouth worked, and clear spittle swelled in it. She realized that he was trying to spit at her, but because of some loss of physical or emotional control he only dribbled it down his chin. He turned, wiped it away with a brisk motion of his tweed sleeve, and said, "When have I ever helped you?" Then he walked off.

~

Annae went home and did not come back to campus. No one seemed to miss her. Her stipend was direct deposited on schedule. Once, there was a call from the dean's assistant, asking if she was all right, and she said yes. After that, she heard nothing.

It seemed to be the end of it all. She spent most of her time mind-reading, latching on to everyone in the little town that she had met, even once: the barista who made the turmeric latte she liked, the department librarian, the firefighter who had dragged her from the rubble of the building. Through their eyes, she watched Brandford renew itself, demolish some ruins and shore up others; she watched the full winter fall on the hiking trails. From her own window she saw the snow, nature's cover-up or concealer. After a while, she began to go out again, her mood oddly light, now that she knew it would be impossible to achieve anything she had ever wanted, now that she knew she was capable of a kind of violence she had never previously imagined. The streetlight was pink, and she aspirated thin winter air and looked at the layers of ruined footprints in the snow. She stockpiled pills, but made no immediate plans to use them. Someday, someone would expel her from the university, but it all seemed very far away compared to the tiny things she was crocheting, and the rashes and moles and even small melanomas she could now raise and smooth away on her skin, and the gnawing, gnashing, crushing force of the shame she felt.

In the darkest moments, she thought of contacting Ariel, but she knew he would only try to help her, and the humiliation of having asked him once was already too much to bear.

~

She'd had no intention of having anything to do with Marec ever again, but then the librarian got sick and went to London to live with her daughter, the barista likewise moved away, and the firefighter went back to their regular gig in Brighton, and in her shaking desperation to remain outside of her body whenever possible, she had to turn to her old classmates. Her favorite was Thomas, a bland boy of angles who spent most of his time and money on drugs, which meant that occupying his mind often provided a feverish blast of ecstasy or energy or sleepiness, like the rivers of color and sparkle that were used in advertisements to show the effects of fruity candy. One day, without warning, she found Thomas in Marec's last seminar.

~

Thomas was hungry and tired; he had been up all night on speed purchased in a dorm toilet from a man named Midge, and now the process was just about over. Marec closed his briefcase and opened his mouth.

"Magic has remained etymologically a shame for millennia. Old French magic, *Latin* magic, *Greek* magic, *Old Persian* magush. *What does this suggest about human beings?" He*

paused, disgust palpating his mouth. "What does this suggest about human beings?"

He took off his jacket, and Thomas saw that the shirt underneath was drenched and brilliant with sweat, the undershirt visible, thick cords of cotton around his arms and neck. Despite himself, Thomas was impressed by this; it was rather punk. When Marec opened his mouth next, a solid, clear wetness poured from the full width of it. Thomas couldn't tell what it was, and Marec paid it no mind, but took a sloppy slurp of his tea.

"What does this suggest about human beings?" he added.

"That we've always known what magic is," said Torquil, half to himself.

"Shut up, Torquil." Marec finally wiped his chin (and was it spittle or something else? Thomas finally wondered, because it had looked more like tears). "At the end I talk about how to be new. How to be fresh, like a flower torn up and nailed to a wall. How that's what you all need to think about, but I've seen no evidence"—a sudden choking—"that, gh-hhsh, you ever have. That's the one real question I've ever asked you, and you act like it means nothing. Do you have any idea how hard I've cried?"

He stooped, braced his hands on his thighs. Then he lost consciousness and never regained it.

~

Annae read him once or twice when he was in his coma. She liked it so much that she stopped after the second time, for fear she'd never come back again.

~

Blackness, muffled songs, a blanket like love, Ariel's voice from a long distance, promising him something. The air in his chest being let in and out, keeping perfect rhythm. Light and warmth, a soft, crisp world where all anyone wanted to do was make him comfortable.

~

She knew when he died, because suddenly the whole town felt beautiful. Even in the dimness and near-terminal hush of her mood, she could tell that his absence had changed things. She went outside and found the leaves hung like earrings on the trees, stirring in a gentle wind. The clouds were breath-soft, as if placed there, and years of pent-up summer cascaded through the streets like a flood, melting the snow. Everyone felt it, those who knew Marec, and those who didn't know him but knew that something was different and better, that the earth sprang back eagerly after their feet sank into it, that suddenly it felt just fine to take off their shoes in the grass of the park, and they weren't worried about whether they'd get dirty. People bought little luxuries in the shops. They spoke more easily, without tension, to their lovers and children. They felt less weird about the concept of "self-care." Smokers quit. Annae cried, because the feeling of benefiting this way from someone's death was awful, and because most feelings had become awful before she'd even left San Cipriano. She was sorry for Marec, she was sorry for Torquil, and she was sorry for herself. Each of these pities was as unfamiliar as the last.

~

The day Ariel came back, she was sitting in a café, staring at her laptop screen. It was a blustery day, the winter having descended again in force, but the previous week's wash of heat was still locked in the stones of the town and you could still smell its leftover breath. The barista had a knitting pattern spread over the surface of the bar and was passing drumming fingers over its crisply unfolded surface, his bag of yarn close at hand with two wooden needles protruding like chopsticks. He regarded the bag as if it were a delicious meal he was about to eat. Annae saw Ariel outside and then he was inside, his thin, benign face looking tired, wrinkles pinched into the spots beneath his eyes. His scarf, she could tell, was real Burberry.

The barista stood up and away from the pattern and made a cappuccino to Ariel's crisp specifications, and he went over to Annae.

~

"Annae," he said. "We only seem to meet in coffeeshops. May I join you?"

She looked up at him, aware that her eyes were large and damp with anxiety, feeling in the moment that this was a very manipulative thing for her body to do. "Oh— God, Ariel. Yes. I'm sorry I haven't— I mean, I'm sorry for your loss."

"Thank you," said Ariel, pulling back the chair and putting his coffee down on the table. "Thank you, that's very kind. It's quite painful, but perhaps no more painful than losing a parent you didn't love."

"You didn't love Marec?"

"I ask my clients to be honest. I try to be honest too. I feel dreadfully sorry for him. And he gave me a sense of profound embarrassment and shame. That's all. Did you call my friend? About therapy?"

"No. I didn't want to take advantage."

"Why don't you want my help? Why does nobody want my help?"

The words were a blank fired from a gun, or that was

what it felt like: a sudden bang, and you weren't dead, but you felt you should be. In a sudden movement he gathered up his bag and scarf, which were still in his lap, and said, "Never mind."

"No, stay—"

"I'm having a long day," he said. "I shouldn't have sat down. I was on my way—to get a look at the body."

He was looking down, his eyes and mouth open, as if using gravity to knock something out of them. Then he seemed to recover himself, and sat back up, and she was reminded that he was dry where others were damp. There were gentle gaps in everything: his conversation, his focus. He said, "Help is a fine thing, Annae. I don't blame you for not taking it—that's not how it works— but my dear, what are you going to do?"

"Don't worry about me," she told him. "I'm all right. I don't miss him."

"You must try."

"Well, trying wasn't working for me," she said, her voice a little raised. "I tried, I went to see you, and then Marec knocked half the city down. I tried, I asked him for help, and then he fucking died. I'm going to try *not* fucking helping, not fucking doing anything, or maybe I'll— I don't know—just leave me alone, please."

She was shocked by her own vituperation, by the sharpness of her voice, and she could tell that Ariel was hurt. He gathered up his things and murmured a goodbye, and then he leaned forward and gripped her shoulder lightly, moving slowly so as to give her plenty of warning. She felt his warmth even through her coat. Then his gentle face was gone, and he had left his coffee on the table.

~

Ariel put his hands into the pockets of his blazer and inhaled Brandford air: thin and cold and astral, winter leaves falling through it without much regard for gravity. Things defied gravity all the time in Brandford. He felt a bit light-headed himself.

Annae's face had been closed, as shut as a prison door, and he knew he would think of it as he tried to sleep that night. He remembered being Marec, remembered hurting people like this, and he thought once again of how the making of him had freed Marec from all shame.

Everywhere in Brandford, he found the memory of his own creation, when he'd still been a half-awake homunculus, with no sense of his place in the world. Marec had been his first person, of course, and he'd had some of Marec's memories, but they were inaccessible, because there were no sensory associations—no remembered smell of gingerbread, no sound of rustling leaves—to recall them to mind.

All he'd really known about Marec was how unhappy he

was. The man would burst into tears sometimes. Ariel, years later, would read an essay by Amy Lowell about the word "daybreak," and how shocking, how avant-garde it must have been when first used, and he felt the same way about "burst into tears": to burst, to swell up and explode. When Marec finished, his nose would be red and distended, the way other people's noses got with drink. Sometimes he would lay his head in Ariel's lap and stare into the fireplace. He would tell Ariel where to sit so that he could do it. He seemed to see Ariel as a technological invention more than anything else, a robot servant, or even a sexbot—that subtext was never far from the surface, although it also never burst through sloppily to the exterior of the water, in which you were suddenly not swimming but wet. Ariel felt terribly sorry for him, and sensed that Marec couldn't show this misery to anyone else, this screaming-baby helplessness. Perhaps witnessing it was the only reason that Ariel had been created. Later, he learned that he had been created so that Marec wouldn't feel unhappy anymore at all. By then, Ariel had accessed the memory of how to drive, and he had gone to London in a little green Saab that Marec hadn't tried to get back.

～

"Miss, are you okay?"

Annae's mouth tasted of blood, and when she opened

it, a line of it welled down her chin. "Shit," she said, or rather "fit," and she bolted to the bar to get a napkin. The knitting barista, his first row half cast on, handed her a stack of them.

"I bit the inside of my mouth," she told him through the blood.

"Are things okay with you and that guy?"

"I'm okay." The trickle of blood was ending; she took her wad of bloodied scarf and cardigan and laptop bag, and passed onto the street.

~

Ariel didn't know how to find the coroner. He sat on some church steps to try to regather his thoughts, the cold of the brown stone drifting up through his bottom. Wasn't he family, anyway? Surely someone would tell family the autopsy results. Surely someone had cut his head open, to have a look at that last gasp of stroke, the bubble of air escaping into some frigid medical room with a disappointing sound.

To the hospital. He'd make his case in the hospital.

Some people have to explain themselves again and again to doctors. Many of Ariel's patients were chronically ill—he had made an accidental specialty of them, as they'd recommended him to one another—and they talked to him about this a lot. Now that he was attuned to it, he saw it in his own life as well. Whenever he sat on the papery table, he felt that familiar dread of having to tell his story whether he wanted to or not—to explain that he had been born twenty-eight years ago, that he had had no boyhood or boyhood diseases, that he wasn't sexually active and had no desire to be, but that he fell in love with men in sudden gut-bubbling ways for reasons he wasn't sure were related to Marec. Then he had to explain Marec. Then he had to explain "gut-bubbling": just what it sounded like, like a bubble, popping painfully inside. A fresh and eager feeling, always very quick, always centered around a dream of holding the other man, tightly clothed, so that his warm system of a body was very close.

Anyway, Ariel was a fully formed person, with a person's normal organic diseases, dyspepsia, pimples, shaved-off bits of skin. He needed to have his stress tested and his heart heard. But explaining himself to each new doctor exhausted him. If they were morbid—and he found that most doctors were—then they knew about homunculi from insomniac nights online, the same way they knew about Cotard's syndrome and the Mary Celeste. It takes a leap of faith, however, to understand that there is a mental illness that makes people believe they are dead, that there was a ship called the Mary Celeste whose crew vanished, that a few magicians per generation create human beings out of their own self-hatred. For Ariel, there was always a quick feeling out, a flourishing of credentials, and a spike in blood pressure that had once *landed him in the emergency room. And for all of these rea-sons, he was afraid of hospitals.*

But he went to the University Hospital of Brandford any-way and spoke to the people at the front desk. He was placed in a little cubicle-room with a baffle ceiling, and a doctor came in and talked him through the autopsy report.

"It was a tumor the size of a cricket ball," said the doctor, the most generic possible young white man—God, how young, barely formed eyes, how had Ariel walked the earth for a similar amount of time? Ariel felt ancient in the morn-ings, dry and tight, and always had to have a bath.

"Do you really measure them by ball?"

"Well, no, but it was—reminiscent of one. I'm sorry." The doctor reddened. "It was of an unusual color. Not to say that any of them are usual. They're all different textures, shapes, levels of solidity. Some have tendrils. Some are soft. They're all essentially tissue that goes mad, so there's no predictable format."

"Not depression of the tissue. Not schizophrenia of the tis-sue. Just madness of the tissue?"

"Well—certain themes and patterns do recur."

"I'm sorry. I'm a psychologist, and I don't like it when peo-ple just say 'mad.'" Aware that this wasn't helping him, Ariel cleared his throat. "I really am terribly sorry. People reported strange events—flows of fluid from his mouth, and so forth. I'm not a magician, but—he called me before he died, and I

honestly have to tell you, he blamed another magician for his death. One of his graduate students. I don't think there was any sense in it, he was very paranoid, but can't you reassure me?"

"About the fluid?"

"It sounds more magical than biological in nature."

"There's no separating magic from biology, Dr. Górski. Any more than you can separate electricity. We think that the tumor disrupted his glandular system."

"You're saying it was just saliva?"

"Yes. Undignified, but most of us don't get dignity." The doctor's flush deepened to brick red. "It may have been developing for years. Unfortunately, he lived alone—had no close friends—so the only people in any position to notice changes were his students."

"And he addressed those mainly by rote, and harshly."

"That's the understanding we got."

"I don't like to go by Górski," said Ariel, into the silence that ensued. "Or doctor, although I am one on paper." A pale and hearty thought: No, Doctor Górski is the man who boiled me up out of the dregs of his personality. Call me Ariel. *He pushed it down and went on with what he'd meant to say. "I've always felt that we shouldn't dilute what being a doctor means. Your work is too important for that."*

"My goodness, no," said the doctor, unmoved. "I'm just a cook, one who works with very low temperatures and very

sharp knives. I failed absolutely to help Marec. What do you go by? It's just that Górski was the name you gave at the desk, sir."

"Just Ariel is fine."

"Ariel. I'm sorry."

"Thank you for taking the time to explain this. And I'm sorry he was difficult. I'm sure he was difficult?"

"He was that," said the doctor feelingly. "He wanted an older man to treat him, but I'm the only oncologist on staff just now. Quite a thing, to spend your last weeks on Earth complaining. Not to say that there's any right attitude for a cancer sufferer—but many people really do reassess and become strangely calm."

"Complaining was Marec's resting state," said Ariel. "Especially after I was excised from him. You mustn't take it personally."

"I try," said the doctor, with a sudden professional smirk, a mask that was horrible mostly because he had gone without it for so much of the conversation. "Do you have any other questions?"

"For years?"

"It wasn't recent," said the doctor. "I can say that with confidence."

~

Isaac Fellman

Ariel found himself back on the street again. He thought about a tumor like a cricket ball, straining in its nest of thready white brain, and he had to sit down on the curb. Cars went by in their wind, and the sun picked out every flaw in the concrete the way Marec had picked out every flaw in him. A fucking cricket ball.

He looked at his skinny ankles in their red socks, a quarter inch of hairy muscle above each one, delicate brown oxfords below. Marec's dress sense, his love of dress, had unexpectedly gone into Ariel along with his love of teaching. He hadn't meant for it to, and had shouted at Ariel for clothing himself with good taste after he'd been conjured from his homely pan of salts and spit. Ariel's first memory was still so vivid, flapping around on the brick floor of the kitchen, his whole body compressed, trying hard to breathe out, or vomit, because the overwhelming desire to get something out of him was the last memory of Marec's that he had. Marec had knelt by him, told him to breathe—in and out!—called him obscenities without regard for grammar, you shit, you cunt, you bollocks, and then Ariel had reached up and fingered the loose fluff of Marec's burgundy turtleneck. It was so soft and beautiful, that pinch of cotton, that he'd wanted to cram it into his mouth, and this had been the thing that had finally made his body uncompress, his mouth open, his lungs work. He was aware of his naked body on the rough brick then, and Marec more tenderly got him up, their four legs wobbling like the

154

legs of a new calf, and brought him to the bedroom, where he'd held the new skin of Ariel's sides between cold protective hands as Ariel dug through the wardrobe for something to put on. He put on wool trousers, a heavy cream shirt, a good wool sweater, and still he was cold. An overcoat, then, of gray tweed. Marec slapped him, then covered his own mouth in a kind of hungry horror, and they turned to each other and embraced, each one aware of something important that was missing. Marec murmured an apology—he had not meant to hurt Ariel—it was just that he had taken Marec's best things—and a little of his warmth finally passed to Ariel, who stopped shaking.

The awful thing about it, Ariel now reflected, was that Marec had not seen the subtext at all, nor been capable of it.

~

Annae came back. She must, she saw, come back. After attuning herself to Ariel's mind as to a favorite song played very quietly under the rattle and roar of an engine, she had not paid attention to where she was walking, and she realized as she returned to herself that she was sitting on a curb too, and that he was sitting on the one across. She gave a limp little wave. He waved back.

~

She went home and rigorously cooked something, a stew with beef sliced through the muscle, properly caramelized onions that took forty minutes to work through, potatoes peeled and sliced small. Her first bowl barely lowered the greasy surface, and she reflected on how goddamn sad it is to cook when you're alone. A splash of grief for Marec came into her mind. The town seemed flatter without him, without its genius loci. *Evil genius,* in the Renaissance sense: a malevolent spirit. The flatness erased shadows and made it easier to move, but sounds also traveled fast and far.

The next morning, when she got up to find breakfast, there was a thick layer of orange grease on top of the stew that made her just close the refrigerator door again.

~

For the funeral: black shirt dress, cut straight; black cardigan with sweater clip in discreet silver bars; nude hose from Waitrose; black oxfords; hair down. No patterns or colors, nothing made by hand. Keys, coins, bus.

She was further relieved to see, in the cathedral of muddy stone with smooth depressions in the rock before each pew, that the mourners were mainly Marec's colleagues. The boy graduate students were sitting in a single row, as if they had arrived together; all of their legs were crossed the same way. She sat down in the back row and regarded Torquil's head, overgrown now at sides and back and with long drooping cowlicks. She sat with her hands in her lap, not wanting to take out her phone.

"He would reliably fuck his students, you know," she heard, and she started because she thought she'd read the phrase without meaning to, but no, it was only two dons behind her, rolling on power wheelchairs into the back aisle. The second don cleared her throat.

"Oh, would you prefer a gentler term?"

"It was 'reliably' that tripped me up, actually, Bernard."

"If you don't use all your words, you'll forget them."

The female don assumed a restful silence, and the male one went on, "It's all due to Ariel. He gave Ariel the romance, but he kept the sex. He told me that three times."

"How did he get them into bed though?" asked the second don in resignation.

"It's not the setup for a joke."

"I'm really asking. How, without understanding romance, did a man who looked and talked like *that* get his students into bed?"

"Oh, he could still turn on the pedagogy sometimes. That did the rest."

"How did you know this?"

"He told me that one twice."

"Well," said the second don after a moment, "I still doubt that he did it *reliably*."

The room quieted, and the service began. At first she paid attention. But her eyes kept being drawn to Ariel, sitting in the front row in the same brown tweeds he'd worn yesterday—but, no, there was a flash at the collar that she had originally mistaken for part of his long red hair. He was wearing a burgundy turtleneck sweater, very soft and old. In this room full of people in black trash bags and rotted weeds, he was dressed like autumn. She reached hungrily into him, her face dissolving into tears as she did so, and this time, she decided that she would not come out again. This was the end of Annae. She was done.

~

The Saab had arrived in London on a Thursday afternoon, that year of Ariel's birth. The city stirred ill-humoredly, despite its beautiful bed. London had no reason to be in such a bad mood. It was the first of November, and Ariel had nowhere to go.

He parked the car by the Thames and crossed the street to the embankment. The river seemed in a bad mood too, slaty and sulky, its waters thick. All of his impressions were clear and sharp as broken glass. He was a new person in a new city. He knew everything Marec knew about life, but he was revolted by all of it.

He sold the car for enough to rent himself a furnished flat for a few months, and strode through it wondering what on earth people did in flats. He had no desire for any pleasures of the flesh, save a few that Marec had missed or forgotten. He loved to comb his hair, for example, and resolved to grow it out long. He loved the feeling of skin in cold sheets; he loved to stretch. And he was wildly bored all the time, of course, because above all Marec had been eager to remove his own capacity for boredom. He used to walk through the flat and just slap everything he saw, experimenting with different textures and different kinds of pain, hungry for a novelty he couldn't define. He went to art galleries and libraries without success. He found an off-the-books job moving crates in the dock-yards, which introduced him to two new sensations—strains and splinters—and gave him enough money to seek professional help. His therapist diagnosed him with depression and ADHD and then discreetly called Marec to confirm that he shouldn't diagnose him with schizophrenia.

In the process of complaining to the board about this grotesque breach of his privacy, Ariel became interested in psychology. Marec hadn't meant to give him any capacity to be interested in anything, but it turned out that by giving him his boredom, he had accidentally given him all of it. He endured a degree of debate about whether he got to share Marec's PhD, and then earned his own PhD. He fell in love with the professor who had taught him how to talk to people soothingly, was rejected, thought about suicide, and decided against suicide.

~

When Ariel came out of his reverie, the funeral service had worn out its ragged groove, and nearly everyone had left. He got up, sore and aching, his neck scratched by the wool turtleneck. Then he turned and saw Annae Hofstader sitting in a pew, looking glossily into space, showing no sign of seeing anybody. Everyone else was leaving, but Annae just sat there in her tidy cardigan, face white and waxen, an inverse silhouette.

The information came to him—quick as a note in a pneumatic tube—that she wasn't there, that her mind was in him. How did he know it? He did not feel her there; he didn't even know what that would feel like. No, it was in the nuance of her expression. Flat as it was, there was a tinge of pity in it, and he recognized the shading: it was the pity he felt.

Ariel had made a great study of pity. In his experience, nearly everybody had either too much of it for themselves or too little. Marec had had too much self-pity, and the Annaes of the world, well, they had almost none. As for Ariel, he thought he generally had too little. It was strange, for he would have expected Marec to give him a good deal of it. But Marec had wanted—more than he himself knew—for

Ariel to be a complete person. Ariel knew that, for he knew what Marec knew, and a good deal more besides. He knew that Marec had wanted to unburden himself, not to burden another. Ariel felt that it is often a kindness to burden another, because everyone needs to be of use, but never mind that; Marec had meant it well. Perhaps it had been the last thing he had ever meant well.

After everyone else was gone, he walked to the back of the church and sat down by Annae's side. She was still staring forward, but he could see the eddies of her expression taking the faint shape of his own. He said, "It's all right, Annae, it's okay. You can come back."

Nothing.

Ariel felt no desire to touch most people. He was a superb therapist partly because he was incapable of transference, of the surge of love, parental or physical, that sometimes attaches to the person who's helping you to feel pain. He felt, now, the electric field that separated him from nearly everyone, but he made himself press through that membrane, made himself put a comforting arm around Annae's shoulders. She still had no reaction. Her nose was running, but she didn't even sniffle.

"I don't know if you know," he said hesitantly, "Marec accused you of killing him. I know that's untrue. If you're feeling ashamed of it, you can let it go."

Nothing.

Ariel sighed and shifted. He gave her shoulder a final awkward squeeze and then let go. He said, "Is there something else? Annae, this is a church, but I am not a priest. I feel as if I'm confessing to you, or you're confessing to me."

Nothing.

"Have *you* anything to confess?"

Nothing, and the distress on her face was only his. He looked down into his lap. Then he got up, more laboriously than he would have liked. He was not old. He had been made less than thirty years ago, and he did an hour of yoga every day, but his body remembered seventy years of life, and that memory—muscles recalling particular bumps and points of stiffness, water flowing through an increasingly obstructed streambed—hobbled and impeded him more than any real aging would have.

He looked around the church for something to use to hurt himself. He did it theatrically, knowing he didn't really want to do this. Nothing. But he knew Annae would do anything to stop someone else harming themselves—he remembered the ouroboros and its tail—and right now he thought it might be the only thing that could move her.

He took a flying leap at a column, but by reflex he found himself grabbing it for support rather than letting it slam into his face. He settled for beating the flat of his arm against it, and was rewarded with a shocking pain, but Annae sat as before.

"You must stop this," he told her. "You must!" It was as effectual a line as Ariel had ever said, which wasn't very. He sat back down again beside her and beat his head against the pew in front, slowly, steadily, in a building rhythm, thunk, thunk, thunk. At first he couldn't get any good pain out of it, but after a few thunks he became very tender and his courage grew. There was a peace in this, a peace in simply letting the red-and-purple pain bloom, testing the drumlike resonance of his skull. He was beginning, even, to enjoy it.

~

"Oh my God, stop," said Annae, and she forced him up with her arms around his chest. His head stayed bowed, fixed in that position, as if he were setting up for another battering. He smelled like clean skin, and he was crying.

He cried for the next quarter hour, unable to properly breathe. He kept coughing deeply, wetly, his chest filling up with mucus and making him cough, as if the tears were going in, not out. Annae held him through it, waited for him to stop, found that he wouldn't stop. She went out of the church to a boba shop she'd seen in the square, got him a hot green tea mixed with hot lemonade and lychee juice, and brought it back to him. He was sobbing and rocking, still moving his head as if to hurt it, but without connecting. She put the drink to his lips. He sipped, and then with a surprised look like a baby's, appeared to take real comfort from it.

"My God," she told him, "I really did believe I'd done it. I've done other things—horrible things."

"What does it even matter how he died?" he said, his eyes as wet and red as his hair. "Of course, it matters to you, and to the law, I suppose. I'm glad he was wrong about being murdered. But I can't stop thinking about the simple fact that he's dead. I'm the only one who has these early memories now. And the rest of his life is just gone."

"How does it feel?"

Ariel took a deep breath into his wet lungs. She watched the soft line of his chin tilting up toward the nave. "Despite my name, I was always more of a Caliban."

"Well, people always name their children after something they want for them. Mine wanted me to be unique, even though they didn't like it when it turned out to be true."

"They also name their children sometimes after something they want to be."

"You think he wanted to be ethereal? Beautiful, a perfect servant?"

"So much that he had to make me, yes. There are so many ways to be beautiful, and he was none of them."

Ariel exhaled sharply, not quite laughing. "How's that for an epitaph?"

Annae took a deep shaky breath, and then she did confess to him. She said, "Ariel, I've hurt somebody really badly. A classmate. A boy who—it doesn't matter. In the earthquake, we were trapped together, and I—I couldn't get out of his mind—he was too anxious. It was too overwhelming. So I did something horrible, without even meaning to. I took his fear out of him, and he changed. I don't even know how he's changed, except that it's bad, and I can't fix it. I don't think I can study magic again. I don't think I can trust myself. But I don't know what else to do."

Ariel took his own long breath and sighed. He sipped his drink through the straw. He said, "At least Marec only took things out of his *own* mind."

"And I'm glad he did," said Annae, "because then he made you."

"Oh," said Ariel, and put down the drink on the pew next to him, almost startled. "Oh, fuck, well. Well." His face crumpled, and he looked ready to cry again, but he did not. He said, "Am I worth it? Was I—really—worth it?"

"You're the only person who's been kind to me in years."

"Now, that's not true," said Ariel.

"Without wanting something for yourself."

"Let's just say I was kind," said Ariel. "Will you do one thing for me? Will you call Bryony Miller?"

"Oh, God, is that what that name was supposed to be?"

"Or literally anybody?" Ariel looked down. "What you did to this young man, was it a crime?"

"Not—well, not in that there's a law against it."

"Then the consequences are between you, only."

"Like I said, I can't even think about talking to him again. I can't imagine he'll ever forgive me."

"Well," said Ariel, "you must forgive yourself."

"Why? I ruined somebody's life."

Ariel's face turned to hers, and in it there was a kind of puzzled pity. He looked, for the first time, like Marec. He said, "If you don't forgive yourself, you will do it again. Not that thing, perhaps, but something as bad. And you must not stop there. You must forgive yourself for all of it, for everything that happened before you did this, both the things that were your fault and the things that were not. You must forgive yourself and do it again, until the very limit of your forgiveness is reached. It will hurt. People don't understand that it hurts. When you have forgiven, you will be able to look at yourself, and then you will be able to change. Not before."

Annae blew her nose on the napkin that had come with the drink. For a moment she could not remember who had wept, herself or Ariel, and she did not know if she would weep now. She had felt Ariel's words as a blow, and although she didn't know if he was correct, the thought of forgiveness was so excruciatingly painful that she knew there was some truth to his words.

She slumped against him and pressed her face to his damp camelhair sleeve, which smelled of wax, as if he burnt candles at home. He let her do it, let her sink deeper into the forgiving fabric as if she could go through it into his skin. She breathed into it for a long time, feeling the steam of her own breath warming and softening her face. Then he shifted away, and she met his eyes as he stood up. He shrugged off the coat and handed it to her.

"I somehow feel that this will help," he said.

She put the coat on. It was warm, and warm from him. They stood there and looked at each other, and then they walked out of the church.

Epilogue

The Society for Neuromancy had its worldwide conference every four years, and this year, 2040, it was in Portland, Oregon. The magicians rode up and down the aerial tram at OHSU, and some of them, who were young and sassy and multidisciplinary, came back after hours to ride on top of it, driving it with electricity from their fingertips. Others ate at food carts in the distant outskirts of the city, craft beer and fish-flavored crisps and strange nests of honey and crackersticks. Dr. Annae Hofstader stayed home at night.

She had come to the conference on the University of Warwick's dime, although her paper proposal had not been approved. She had come early, to help clean out her mother's house, but then had given up and contracted with an estate sale company. Now the young Portlanders, wearing precious iridescent shell jackets from the 1980s, were tidying her mother's shelves and stripping clean her closets. They would glean the house clean like birds on a bone. Annae went to the conference.

Toward the end of day two, she was thumbing the

scheduling app. People streamed around her through the hall, toward the student posters or the VR therapy demonstration. Unconsciously, she pulled at the throat of her coat, making the bubble of cloth a little tighter around her, becoming smaller but also more contained.

Someone brushed against her, shoulder-checked her really, and she turned to apologize or start something depending on the expression on the man's face, but then she met a face with no expression: Torquil Gibson's.

He had aged very little, from a prematurely old thirty to a very young fifty. The reddish-brown hair had receded, that was all. His face had the beseeching cast of some terminally relaxed people, in which the face loosens, the eyes fall open. There was nothing aggressive in his posture.

"Torquil," she said, and her hand went again to her collar.

"Is it Annae?" he asked quietly, not really asking. The words seemed an echo from somewhere else. She glanced reflexively at his nametag, saw TORQUIL GIBSON, and underneath a ribbon that said KEYNOTE.

"I didn't know you were even here."

"I didn't know you were even alive," he said.

"How did I not know you did work in my field? When are you speaking?"

"Oh, I already did. At the luncheon. I'm not in the

program. The person who was supposed to speak had an emergency, and they tapped me." He cleared his papery throat. "I do some work now—on absence of empathy. Work with a therapist. Treating people who've got no empathy by teaching them magic skills. That's where the plants come in. I can still feel quite caring toward plants."

"Oh, I see."

"My talk was about how you don't need magic to live well."

"Do you believe that?"

"No." He looked at her again with dry eyes. "I'm sorry I ran into you. With the coat on—from the corner of my eye—I thought you were someone else."

"No, you didn't."

"No," he said. "I didn't."

"I don't know that we have anything to say to each other."

"If you don't know," he said, "then why speculate aloud?" He lifted his head slightly, and the motion reminded her very much of Marec. "Is Himself here? Jonathon Bayer?"

"God knows. I don't think so. I can't spend all day keeping tabs on my exes."

"You know—I could've been your ex."

"Is that something you think about a lot?"

"Sometimes," he said. "We do share a dreadful secret.

Isn't that what being an ex means?"

"Oh, God, I don't know." She loosened her grip on her coat. "Torquil, I'd invite you for coffee and catch-up, but I think we'd better not."

"Agreed. Are you well?"

"No, but—Torquil—I've done good work."

"Are you still fixing the anxieties of mice? Or by now are you up to macaques?"

"No. I'm teaching," she said. "Mostly."

"Really?"

"I'm a very good teacher, Torquil. I learned from the worst. And I promised myself I wouldn't let anyone be failed as I was failed." She paused, looked him in the eyes, thought better of going on. Ariel's coat made a protective warmth around her.

"Huh. Well—people surprise you," he said noncommittally. Then they parted, and he passed off toward the exhibition hall.

Acknowledgments

I'm grateful to my agent, Kate McKean, and my editor, Christie Yant, for making this book possible. Melanie Sanders was an able copyeditor, and FORT provided the lovely cover. Waverly SM gave me useful details about the UK higher education system, as well as the great honor of their love and companionship.

About the Author

Sarah Jung

ISAAC FELLMAN is the author of *Dead Collections* as well as *The Breath of the Sun* (published under his previous name), which won the 2018 Lambda Literary Award for queer science fiction, fantasy, and horror. He is an archivist at the GLBT Historical Society.

TOR·COM

Science fiction. Fantasy. The universe.

And related subjects.

*

More than just a publisher's website, *Tor.com*
is a venue for **original fiction, comics,** and
discussion of the entire field of SF and fantasy,
in all media and from all sources. Visit our site
today—and join the conversation yourself.